Quickies /kwi-kk-eez/

1. Noun :
   a one night stand.

   ✓ Ronnie's resolution is to hook up with as many hot chicks as possible, and quickies are the only way to go.

2. Verb :
   a quick puff of the joint.

   ✓ While DJ swam in the thoughts of the beer pitcher he had just emptied, the others hit heaven with a hash quickie.

Forget the meaning of the word. The rules will make you the king of playboys. ;)

Other Quickies you can pick:

Daring Daroga: Killer in the Shadows!

Inspector Abhay Pandey, Uttar Pradesh Police, is a man of simple deeds - *Haseeno ko bachaana, gundon aur politicians ki bajaana. Fir chhamiya party mein nachna-gana.* When a mysterious murder points the finger towards the next victim, Naina – the one with the beautiful eyes – our Daring Daroga will leave no stone unturned to find the killer and save the belle.

Dark Temptation: The Naughty Proposal!

Two strangers meet and kindle desires long repressed. Then they meet again and explore some more. Without the shackles of a relationship binding them down, they indulge in sinful pleasures, amorous games and unbridled passion. Will they end up in love? Or are they in for a surprise?

Criminal Masterminds: Catch Me? No You Can't!

Raja Tiwari is freshly out of jail, and not just because of stealing hearts and killing with his looks. He is looking for a new job, and lands up in one, topped with a silky bonus. With ex-cop Thakur, and the sexy Silky Sinha, he has to pull a task that could make him rich or land him back behind bars. Will he play his angle and beat everyone else to the end?

10 RULES OF F**G AROUND

Vicky Arora

Quickies

Srishti Publishers & Distributors
N-16, C. R. Park
New Delhi 110 019
editorial@srishtipublishers.com

First published in Quickies by
Srishti Publishers & Distributors in 2015

10 9 8 7 6 5 4 3 2 1

The story begins in a large duplex bungalow in Anand Niketan in South Delhi, which I shared with my friend DJ. We would have had to sell ourselves to afford living in such a swanky place, if our fathers were not such big shots in Chandigarh. So, the money kept pouring in for both of us from our parents. DJ moved into the bungalow a week before me, and thankfully took care of everything we might need. Apparently this bungalow belonged to his father's friend, or was bought from his father's black money…one of those. But I didn't care.

It was just cool that we both ended up here. With DJ around, I felt like I already had a built-in support system. When he showed me this luxurious independent bungalow, I attached myself to him like a Siamese twin and was happy to share the rent. This place was awesome. I could come home with seven different girls every day, and no one would bother to notice me.

By the way, DJ is short for Diljit Singh, but that had last been heard sometime in school. I was one of the few people who knew that and I was sworn to secrecy. He said pretty girls found him more interesting with just the initials. I had little faith in that theory, but I kept it a secret nonetheless.

The bungalow was pretty close to the Delhi University campus and hot chicks could be seen by the dozens, without too much effort. So I sat on the cold marble slab at the window and enjoyed the eye candy. I also watched happy couples come and go, hand in hand. I used to call them '*chingam couples*' because they would stick to each other like chewing gum even if there was no taste left in the gum.

I never understood why some guy would want to choke himself by being with just one girl. I called such guys '*footiyas*'. Actually a *footiya* is a guy who goes to an ice cream shop if his girlfriend says 'I like chocolate flavour' and not to the chemist. I didn't want a girlfriend, not really, at least not right away. But I would love to have someone warm my bed. It had been a while since I'd had a chance at it, and my Bull kept reminding me how warm it wanted to be.

God, what a whiner I was! I reminded myself that I was one lucky son-of-a-bitch living a pretty fucking cool life, and my grumbles, compared to most people's in the world, were so minimal and stupid and small, it was incredible I even bothered with them. I watched a bird land on the tip of a lamppost across the street. It fluttered its wings, teetered, fluttered again, and finally found its balance. "That's me," I told myself. "I'm just like that bird. Flying from one lamppost to the other."

Then something deep inside me asserted itself. "What the fuck are you talking about?" I muttered, then half-laughed aloud. God, maybe I had my period.

Saturday was winding down, and the lampposts sparkled to life. It was early November and the Delhi winter had not set in completely, not yet. As the sun finally set, a cool breeze informed me that it was going to be a cold night. I wondered where my hash was. It just seemed like something that might help right now. I stared at my iPhone contacts and stopped at QD's – the *adda* for students for its tandoori momos. I would call QD's in a while, like I always did, for my tandoori momos. It was getting a little embarrassing, though.

"Hello, QD's."

"Hi, I want to place a home delivery order."

"Hi sir...*aap samney first floor sey bol rahe ho na*?"

"Um, yeah."

"Chicken clear soup and tandoori chicken momos with extra red chutney? Correct, sir?"

"No, um, today I think I will try the veg option."

"Sir, are you sure?"

"Fine. Give me the chicken."

"Okay. Fifteen minutes, Emraan sir."

They may have known my voice, but they'd never know my name. They somehow thought I was Emraan, the Bollywood guy who always gets a girl in every movie he does. I think he was the only guy after James Bond who got a girl for no reason.

So I wasn't Emran. I was Ronnie Kapoor, a Punjabi guy from Chandigarh. Ever since I moved to New Delhi two years ago, I had used pseudonyms when ordering in. Wood Box Cafe, my second most frequent home delivery restaurant, knew me as Ricky Bahl – the guy who could play with three girls in the movie and still get away with it.

I slipped back into the white wicker chair lying near the window and began weighing options for the evening. Common sense held that I should eat my dinner, watch a porn movie like most single guys, and get a reasonable night of sleep before the next day.

But my Bull, my damn Bull. He just wouldn't shut up. And I had to admit, his argument wasn't without merit, or logic. His basic premise: "Any girl out tonight might be just as desperate as you." I offered that I had been out a lot this week; the last two nights hadn't ended until way into the morning, and even now a slight hangover hummed in my head. But Bull, as I called him, was influential. The problem with being a boy is the constant struggle between listening to your brain and listening to your Bull. The problem with being me was that somehow my Bull had acquired the argumentative skills of a lawyer. Or perhaps, my brain was an equal party with it.

I took a quick shower and had just barely gotten a towel around me as the doorbell rang, announcing the arrival of my evening snacks. I opened the door and handed a Bahadur a few crinkly currency notes in exchange for his one crinkly bag. I quickly pulled on a pair of comfy jeans and a red sweat shirt that read: "Man has three sizes - Large, XL and Oh my God". Who cared about the others? I was proud of my size.

After eating straight out from the boxes – yummy, same to same taste – I went back into the bathroom and fussed with my hair a bit. I flaunted the same short-ish, messy-ish style that every guy thought made him look cool. I looked around for my lucky charm glasses, and cursed myself for keeping the room so dirty when I couldn't find them. My zero power glasses, real cool ones – red stems and black frame. Not that I had some eyesight problem, but the first night I had gone out with my glasses on, I had made out with a deliciously hot girl. Call me superstitious, but I was so damn sure it worked!

When I finally found them beneath a pile of dirty clothes, DJ's message got delivered on WhatsApp. *Come to Matchbox lounge, Hauz Khas village. Happy hour night tonight. A new band Toya performing live tonight. I have heard they are good. See you there.*

It was almost eight. I twisted a joint, opened a beer can and let them race each other to see which could get to my brain first. For me, beer and hash went together like milk and Bournvita. Like Emraan Hashmi and kiss. Like Ricky Bahl and three girls. I hit the lights off, locked my door, and let gravity take me down the stairs, though the joint was helping me defy gravity really nicely. Once I was outside, the cool night air felt great against my skin. *By God ki kasam, feeling aa gayi badi sahi.*

I walked towards the autorickshaw stand a few metres away from my home. I pulled out my iPod, ear-phoned up, and clicked PLAY. The popular song by Yo Yo Honey Singh "Party All Night" came on and that set the mood to 'party'. I turned it up loud enough to drown out the rest of the world. My steps began unconsciously landing on the beat, my hands were slapping at my sides like they were a percussive instrument.

I was stoned and easily distracted. Plus, I didn't want to fly off on a tangent. So I tried to concentrate on my mission. I was going to see this Toya band. They might just become my new favourite band. Maybe I would buy a T-shirt and start a blog on the band name Zoya or whatever the name was. The hash kick had begun!

Going to a bar alone might not be a big deal for some people, but for me it was always a bit of an awkward experience. Somehow it always felt as if everyone were looking at me.

"Did he come by himself?"

"Did he get stood up by a girl?"

"Is he gay and here to pick up a waiter?"

It had happened with me many times. DJ had gone missing and I had to stand people's looks. But then, after a while, I learnt not to care.

Clubbing wasn't something I did often, but I liked the adventure attached with it. The hash took care of the slight anxiety and made me feel like the funniest guy to ever roam the planet. Though once inside the bar, it sometimes gave me the inner confidence of a man whose fly was stuck open. But that's ok, isn't it!

I waved at an autorickshaw that stopped immediately. I hopped and told him to drive towards Hauz Khaz village. The exotic-smelling autorickshaw driver started ranting. "Sirjee, do you do a job? It looks like you do a job. Most people I pick up are stuck in some job which they don't like and they have to listen to their boss." I think he mistook my doped out face for an employee working under some stupid boss. I just gave him a dirty look that clearly said "shut up!" But he seemed hell bent on blabbering.

"Sirjee, I love my work. I am my own boss and nobody tells me what to do."

Then I replied, "*Bhen ke laude, aage se left le le.*"

Luckily, when I arrived at Matchbox, the band was already playing, so I felt like just another guy who had come to check them out. Matchbox was a large bar with a small stage, very popular for its draught beer. I made my way toward the only empty stool. I climbed aboard and ordered a lager beer.

I looked around for DJ, but he was nowhere to be seen. I checked the crowd out: men, men, boys, boring women, boring women, ugly women, badly dressed women...none to wake the Bull up. Perhaps some office team had come for some fucker's farewell, adding to the usual mix of young students, mostly from south campus colleges. I moved my shoulders and rolled my neck to ease the tension out. I had a hint of a headache and the beer wasn't really helping matters...yet.

As I was sipping my beer, a girl squeezed herself smoothly between me and the guy on the next stool, shouting on top of her voice, "Rohan, Rohan…!" Either she knew this Rohan guy in the band or she just liked to yell randomly. I checked her out: glasses similar to mine, straight and shiny hair, smooth skin and long, pretty fingers. She held her money up to the bartender. The bartender overlooked, but my Bull stirred.

There is a thin line between 'love at first sight' and 'lust at first sight', and the line is called 'cleavage'. She was definitely flaunting it well, and Bull fell for it. Actually Bull stood for it.

I saw the girl struggling for a vodka. *By God ki kasam, bahot pareshan thi kanya kunwari.* It was my duty to help her *yaar.*

"I'll help you get the drinks?" I told her over the music.

She was shocked with my offer at first. But then my glasses worked their charm and she smiled. "Thanks, could you ask the bartender for a Grey Goose Vodka, please?" She handed me the money.

I took her money. "Oh ji, no problem." Just a single drink, she was probably here alone. My Bull was triumphing already. Getting a drink in the busiest of the bars in just five seconds was my forte. It had needed some practice, but I knew I had this under control now. I made eye contact with the bartender, who had known me to be generous with the tips in the past. He left everyone and came and took my order.

> **Rule 1: Make the right contacts at the right places. It always helps you make the first impression.**
>
> **Whether you are at a restaurant, a pub, a library or a movie theatre, always make it a point to find the right guy and make him your man by giving a generous tip, or a smile or a pat on the back.**

The bartender leaned in.

"Grey Goose vodka please," I said, smiling at him.

"On the rocks or you need a mixer?" He smiled.

"On the rocks please," she said. The bartender fixed it and I gave the cutie the change.

"I'm Ruchika," she said to me, holding up her drink.

"Ronnie." I clinked her glass with the huge beer mug which was now almost empty. "Nice to meet you."

As she smiled and said, "Same here", the band took a break and the DJ started playing Punjabi rap songs The disc jockey, not my friend DJ. Ruchika started telling me about her love for music and how she hated the latest Punjabi rappers who sang songs full of abuses.

"I don't know how people can enjoy such songs? They have no meaning."

I just nodded. It was difficult to lie. For the love of Punjab, I loved every single Punjabi rap song by Honey Singh. Especially the censored ones which were released only online. *By God ki kasam, kitney meaningful hotey hain yaar yeh gaaney. Jab tak do teen ma bhen na ho, mazaa kahaan aata hai.* There's no kick without swearwords!

She liked my acceptance of her views and flashed me a grin, perfect teeth wet with vodka which reminded me of the song "*Chaar botal vodka, kaam mera roz ka*" but I controlled myself.

We chatted for a while, and the songs grew louder and louder. She had gulped in around seven glasses of vodka on the rocks and was tipsy enough for me to be happy. The disc jockey played the song "*Aaj botlan khullan do, daru sharu dullan do, party all night*". She got up and started dancing. And I wanted to tell her that these were the same songs she had been cursing till a few minutes back. But how could I let go of this golden opportunity!

I waived to her and went to the bar to fetch us more drinks.

"Hey, do you want to go somewhere else?" She held her almost-full glass up to mine. "I mean, after these?"

"Sure. I mean, maybe in a while." I wonder what time was it.

I was enjoying the drink and checking her out. She was wearing a cut-sleeved T-shirt with Babe written in all caps on the front, with a short denim skirt and sandals. If those sandals could talk, I guessed they'd probably say something like, "Look out for that cow dung!" or something. Yeah, sandals didn't seem like they'd have much of a personality. Those high boots girls wore, now those you'd want to sit next to at a party. They knew the secrets of the back of the knee.

Ruchika went to use the restroom and I looked at her nice back, swinging to a tune of their own. When she was back, I had to go, to reduce the liquid in my system and for some minor adjustments too.

I carefully used my foot to lift the toilet seat. I did my thing and then used my foot again to flush. When it came to using public toilets, I was very particular about using them without touching them with my hands. If only I could manipulate my foot to turn restroom doorknobs, I could live without any fear of bathroom germs. Maybe someday I will be able to lift the lid, flush and open the door by clicking a few buttons on my iPhone.

I found Ruchika dancing near our spot. The crowd had somewhat thinned since we'd arrived. I still wondered what time it was, but then I couldn't care less. She continued dancing and I continued checking her out.

We left when the disc jockey decided to shift the songs to retro mood with '*Jahaan teri yeh nazar hai*'. I had to literally pull her away from her dancing spot. I was not much of a club dancer; I was more into *shadi* dancing. My dance style had brought accolades to me and my family in marriages, and embarrassment to me and my friends in pubs.

We had been out for a couple of minutes and walked towards nowhere in particular. "So what do you want to do now?" she asked.

"Umm, I could get another drink. Maybe at a quieter place," I tried my luck and Bull's.

"I'm kind of hungry," she said, adjusting her skirt. I stopped and looked around instinctively. I couldn't see anything around – any restaurants, or even *dhabas*.

"Well, we could go to my apartment and order in. And if you want, I have some *Babaji ki booty* there." I regretted the choice of words as soon as I uttered them; I must have sounded so B grade. Too late.

"That sounds perfect. I would love to have some hash."

We sat on my small green couch. She finished off a piece of momo while I rolled a joint and grabbed a mug to act as an ashtray. '*Angrezi beat tey*' by Sir Highness Honey Singh was in the stereo; not the sexiest choice, but it was what was already in there when I hit play. I remembered that she had both hated and enjoyed Punjabi songs, so I went with it. She excused herself to go to the restroom, and I flicked the lighter and inhaled some smoke. Instantly I felt it, a small tingling in my ears and a bit of nervous energy. The toilet flushed and my mind began racing with *Babaji ki booty* settling in. This was just too easy. What was up with this girl? What if she rifled through my apartment in the middle of the night and stole my Honey Singh CDs? What if she was a boy? I made a mental note to check both.

She came and sat next to me. I handed her the joint and took a sip from the beer can to shake off the sleepiness.

"So, what have you been up to? I've just been here all day. I mean right here, on this chair by the window. I had a late one last night."

"Oh yeah?" She blew a perfect smoke ring. I'm talking perfect. It hung above her head and rotated, slowly dissipating and softening until it disappeared into the ceiling. She ashed into the mug and looked around my apartment.

She adjusted a pillow behind her back. "I was up very late myself. I was partying almost until five a.m." She exhaled another perfect smoke ring.

"How do you do that?" I said, pointing to it. "I always wanted to be able to blow one of those." I felt like a teenager outside the school, talking to the bad kid.

"You don't smoke, though, do you, Ronnie?"

I shook my head. "Just hash."

She explained rapidly, "Okay, now, while you hold the smoke in your lungs, make an 'O' with your lips. Then let the smoke slowly pool in your mouth. But don't exhale! You have to open your epiglottis thing and just let it go there. Okay? When it's in your mouth, with one quick puff, blow all the smoke out through the O." She made the movement with her lips. I wished she would make the same 'O' shape with her lips at the right place. The moment that thought hit my mind, Bull waggled.

I tried to follow what she was saying but the smoke dribbled out, shapeless. "I have no idea what you are talking about," I half-laughed, half-coughed. I passed the joint back her way.

"You have to keep trying. You really need to have a will to do it." She took a deep drag and then blew a smoke hula-hoop. "Ooh, that's a good one," she said, watching it slowly expand, rotate and then break apart. "It's one of those things where you have to picture yourself doing it successfully, mentally prepare yourself, and then one time, boom, it just all comes together." She shook her head. "Whoa, I'm feeling this already. This stuff is so much stronger than what I had last night. Where did you get it from?"

"Well this is from McLeod Ganj. Last month, me and my friends had gone all the way to bring some good stock. The stuff available here in Delhi is not that good," I said, taking a pull. I tried the ring thing again. *Ghanta, sala ring fir nahi banaa.* I waved my hand through the white cloud.

"Really! You guys went all the way just to buy hash? Hats off to you man!" she said, putting the joint to her lips. It was about halfway gone. She took a short strong drag, blowing the smoke out of her nose.

We started a halting conversation about God knows what, both of us waiting for the inevitable to happen. I put my hand on her leg and took the joint gently from her fingertips. Honey Singh sang "*I swear chhotee dress mein bomb lagdi mainu …*" I started saying something and then, I don't know who started it, but after seconds of leaning closer and closer to each other, we started kissing deeply.

The first trading of tongues officially ended my week of dryness, and I resisted the urge to hop up and perform a victory dance. After what felt like the right amount of time, I gently reached up her top and went on with the artful rubbing of the naughty pieces. It was fun to go down from the top as it helped the girl get comfortable. Once I had tried the bottom to top approach, and the girl had left instantly.

Rule 2: Make your partner comfortable. Start by kissing softly, and slowly move down. As you go down slowly, you will be more acceptable to each other and your partner will believe that you are interested in much more than just sex.

Till now I had thought she was cute, but the definition was changing. She seemed more hot than cute. She had impeccable breasts and I artistically spent time on the canvas in circular rounds.

Ruchika unbuckled my belt and released Bull, who stood at attention. The same thought ran through my mind that ran through my mind every single time I hooked up: "I can't believe this girl is actually going to touch Bull!" Yes, every single time.

After some grappling and half-naked clumsiness, we started towards the bed but never reached it. As she leaned against my closet, I stood behind her and went on with the act. I could hear the contents of my wobbly closet as I fucked her. My favourite puma belt with a metal buckle fell down. I could hear three of my watches hugging each other in fear in the drawer. She looked back at me and snarled, "Is this the best you can do?"

By God ki kasam, ego hurt hogayi Bull ki. I thrust and thrust, pushing deeper and deeper. I made sure she would never say this to anyone else ever again.

I woke up the next morning with a penetrating headache. Besides some lingering nausea, the headache turned the light from the window into needles to the eyes. I slowly stood and made my way out of the bedroom, dragging my feet across the cold floor. I wanted to sleep more but not being the type who could fall back to sleep, I didn't even try. I needed a room which was completely dark and silent. Getting a good sleep was a gift that some people had; they could go back to sleep after waking up, or they could fall asleep in the middle seat on a packed train or on a bus racing along a hill station. I wasn't one of them.

I sensed that Ruchika had opened her eyes and was looking at me, probably trying to remember if I was the same guy who talked to her in the pub the night before. Maybe she was wondering if I'd ever meet her again.

When I walked into the kitchen, I saw DJ sleeping on the floor, propped up against the cabinets and holding a pitcher of beer. I admired his drinking tenacity. He was a big guy with a square face and a strong chin. And definitely a strong liver.

Beer stains speckled his faded blue sweatshirt that said "Textually Active" – he surely was both textually and sexually active. I thought I should wake him up, but then I looked at him. He looked utterly content and happily asleep, so I let him be. *By God ki kasam, bada he pyara lag raha tha zameen par sotey huey.*

The bar flaunted a variety of empty liquor bottles. It always reminded me of the wonderful bar in Supriya's house. I had dated her for some time and we had made some hot to and fro movements near her dad's bar.

It didn't last. The dating, I mean. She, like many other girls seemed to me like Subhash Chandra Bose: '*Tum mujhe commitment doh, toh main tumhe pyaar dungi.*' I was scared of such girls and disappeared at the right time.

I moved to the sink and found it empty. It was the first time I had seen the bottom of the sink since we moved in. I clicked a picture of the empty sink from my iPhone and uploaded it on Facebook. It was a picture worth preserving. I instantly got three likes.

I turned on the tap and stuck my head under it. There was no water!

I grabbed the Maggi cup-o-noodles. I looked for a bowl and found one. The origin of the bowl was a mystery in itself. Neither I, nor DJ had bought these pink bowls. DJ's mom could have bought them for us when she was here on a weekend visit. I'd like to think that, anyway. But I can't help but imagine that there's a girl's apartment somewhere nearby that was suddenly missing an entire set of pink bowls after DJ attended one of their parties.

I picked up the water bottle from the top shelf of the refrigerator; it was empty. I shook it just to make sure there weren't a few drops hiding in there somewhere. Nothing. I returned it to its spot.

Maggi without water wasn't an option. It could have been an option as a starter or *chakhna* with drinks, but never in the mornings. So I reached over and took the pitcher from DJ's hand – a task so herculean that you cannot even begin to imagine.

Warm beer flowed over the maggi and I placed it in the microwave for two minutes. Long ago I had bought into the college myth that more beer in the morning could cure a hangover.

The smell of the beer mixed with Maggi was mesmerizing. As the microwave beeped to a halt, I opened the door of the unit and stuffed the first bite of Beer-o-Maggi in my dehydrated mouth.

I had eaten around twenty-four versions of Maggi at the famous Kev's Maggi shop near Venky college in south campus, and this twenty-fifth version of Maggi Kev's sure didn't have. Maybe I could sell him the idea. As I gulped the second bite; there was a knock at the door.

"Come in," I yelled and a few stray noodles slipped past my lips and onto the floor. The door opened and there stood Bhaskar, dressed in a pair of jeans too blue and a sweatshirt too big.

"Where were you?" I asked. "Why didn't you come to Matchbox last night?"

"I was too tired and slept early," he said, holding up a stupid grin.

"*By God ki kasam,*" *tu bada dhakkan hai yaar.* You missed a kick-ass party last night."

"I wanted to come, but was too tired bhai."

Bhaskar was our cute *padhakoo* friend. The friend who always finished our assignments, gave his Xeroxed notes to us and sometimes even taught us before the exam. He was from Ranchi where his father ran a chemist shop and his mother was a homemaker. His financial situation was not that great, and he stayed in a private boys' hostel right next to Sri Venkateshwara college (which we called Venky with love), which saved him lot of time and money on rentals and travel.

I took another bite of Maggi. The taste of beer made me want to puke, but I was so hungry I kept eating. Bhaskar walked past me into the living room and slumped on the couch.

"What's wrong?" I asked.

"Nothing."

"Come on. What's wrong?"

"Nothing," he said, more convincingly.

"*Bataa na chutiye, dimaag mat chaat.* I don't have the energy right now."

"Seriously, nothing's wrong."

"Okay." I started to count to ten in my head. I was interrupted at seven.

"Girls hate me," Bhaskar said.

I gathered my best conciliatory, semi-monotone voice, almost like Ramdev Baba. "They don't hate you *bachcha*."

"Nobody ever wants to go out with me. I need a girlfriend."

"The last thing you need is a girlfriend. You need to come to parties with me and get laid."

"I don't know why I can't meet anyone. How do you do it?"

"I don't know. You have to get out, man. Don't you meet girls in your classes?"

"No."

"In your hostel?"

"I live in a boys' hostel and you know it," he said.

"Oh, yeah. What about college clubs?"

"I'm not in any clubs and don't even tell me to join a stupid club."

"I wouldn't dream of it," I said. "Are you going to the library today? That can be a good place to meet chicks."

"Actually, I have just recently seen a girl in the college library and I think I am in love. I went to the library around three days back and there she was, sitting and studying. Her name is Aaliya Oberoi. I have been dreaming of her for the last two days, fascinated by the nape of her neck because that's all I see when she looks down to read. Look, I even downloaded her pictures from her Facebook account. Looking at Aaliya Oberoi in her swim suit is the closest thing I can get to sex. Of course, I've never actually spoken to her and she doesn't know I exist. But besides that, I think we have something really special."

This is how Bhaskar always spoke. '*Mein usey jaanta nahin hoon, woh mujhsey kabhi mili nahin hai, par I think mujhe pyar ho gya hai. Bhai kuch help kar na.*'

I shoved in a few more spoons of Maggi and quickly sat down at the table behind the couch. Snatching his phone, I asked, "Who's Aaliya Oberoi? The name doesn't sound like the library types."

The moment my eyes landed on Aaliya Oberoi, my mind took a snapshot of her for later use in shower. Her slightly wet black hair fell just below her shoulders. The angular features of her face were perfectly proportioned – the kind a sculptor would kill for. My eyes traced the lines of her body, currently wrapped in a swimsuit at a beach. *By God ki kasam, kya rapchik bandi hai yaar.*

And that's when something bad happened. A bad feeling washed over me upon seeing Miss Oberoi; a feeling I knew I shouldn't have had. I suddenly knew there was nothing in this world that would make me help Bhaskar get that girl. Because I wanted her for *myself*. Wanting a girl was nothing out of the ordinary, mind you, because I wanted most girls I saw.

But I wasn't supposed to want this one.

Anyway, there she was in all her glory: good looks complete with an attitude. She just kind of, put out that vibe. You know the one I mean. And I knew what that vibe meant for Bhaskar. She was a girl he was never going to get. I think he knew it too, and maybe that was why he was living in his little dream world. If he could have a girl like her, he would be cool. And being cool would lead to other good things that came from that whole "I date a hot girl" effect.

And as I watched Aaliya, the gravity of Bhaskar's situation became clear to me. If he were to ask her out, she would reject him and he would have to face the reality that he would never go out with a girl like her. Or worse, she would say yes because she couldn't come up with a good excuse fast enough, or she thought it would be fun for one date, or possibly because she had absolutely nothing else to do that night. They would go out. Bhaskar would spend the better part of a day worrying about it, getting ready, asking me for advice. That night, he would stumble all over himself trying to impress her while she would wonder why she wasn't out with the captain of the cricket team. They would say good night. He wouldn't try to kiss her because it was the first date, and she wouldn't want him to kiss her for reasons very different. He would think they would go out again, while she would be thankful that the evening was over; happy that she made a new friend, happy that she got free dinner and drinks, and ready to go back to her regular life.

Bhaskar, on the other hand, would be heartbroken beyond what any mortal should suffer when he'd learn that the one he 'loved' had no intention of going out with him again…ever. It would take the rest of the year, all of the next year, some Atif Aslam sad songs and some time in therapy for him to accept his situation in life. Basically, Bhaskar *ki lag gyi thi*. Already.

It's amazing that I could get that much out of just seeing her. Don't you think so too? Sherlock! Sometimes even I surprise myself. I just don't know how I do it.

Bhaskar reached for the television remote. "What do you think?" he asked.

"She looks good."

Of course I couldn't tell him that I thought she was one of the hottest girls I'd ever seen, or more importantly, that she had the capacity to rip out his heart and mash it into the ground and make a potato hash brownie out of it.

I took another bite of my Maggi. I could tell that Bhaskar was waiting for a solution to his girl problem, even though he was pretending to watch *Two-and-a-half Men* on TV. You see I was like Charlie Sheen in that show, who could get any girl, and Bhaskar was like his younger brother who was a big loser.

I didn't really think he had a problem. *I* had a problem now. I tried to pretend I was listening while thinking of a way to change the subject. My head was swimming more than the Maggi, and I couldn't think of anything to say.

There was another knock at the door just as I took a beer-flavoured bite. Bhaskar got off the couch and moved over to the door. He opened it and I saw Prerna standing in the doorway. Only when I saw her did I remember that I had to meet her for lunch. *By God ki Kasam, bahot bajayegi yeh meri.*

Prerna looked really mad. She stormed past Bhaskar and glared at me.

"I was going to come," I said.

"Where were you? I've been waiting for an hour."

"You weren't waiting for an hour."

"Whatever. Forty-five minutes. I am sure you have been screwing around again." Her nostrils were flaring and I had to jump to emergency remedial measures.

"I slept in," I said. "I even set my alarm when I went to bed. I must have turned it off in my sleep."

I lied like a dog. But notice how I didn't say I was sorry. This brings us to the third rule of survival with a girl.

Rule 3: When you realize that you have committed a blunder, simply lie and don't feel sorry. Even if you feel sorry, don't say it out loud or you will lose the battle even before it starts.

Mind you, my rules are not about being nice or doing the right thing. They are about surviving the trials and tribulations that come in your life because of fucking around.

You see, it's very scientific. Usually boys believe what they see, and girls believe what they hear. In fact, that is why boys lie and girls wear make-up.

Prerna rolled her eyes. "Nice boxers." She turned and walked into the kitchen.

I stood up and followed her while I looked down at my red angry bird boxers.

"What's wrong with my boxers?"

She didn't answer. Well, I think she was really angry. Prerna was the only girl out of the hundreds I had known who had been consistently there. Not that we were dating or something. We had eaten many lunches together and also attended parties together when neither of us had a date. She belonged to a middle class family in Moga, Punjab. But I remember clearly, when I had met her here in Delhi, she seemed different than the rest of the girls I had been with. She was modern and watched only English channels, stayed away from *saas-bahu* serials and dressed up like a model with loud colours. There was something different about her.

"Alright, relax!" I said. "I should have been there. Do you want some Maggi?"

"No, I already ate. Remember?"

"Okay."

Prerna peered into my bowl. "Is that beer? Did you put beer in your Maggi?"

"Yeah. You know, my head is killing me. Could you not talk so loud?" *By God ki kasam, kitna chey chey kar rahi hai.*

She snatched the bowl out of my hands and dumped it into the dustbin. "What's wrong with you? Use water." She threw open the refrigerator door and grabbed the water bottle. "This is empty."

"I know. Doesn't that suck?"

She put the empty bottle back in the refrigerator.

I tossed my arms up in disbelief. "You're not going to throw it away?"

"Yeah, like I'm going to start throwing away your garbage."

"Fair enough."

"Oh God, go take a shower. What have you guys been doing anyway? Why is DJ sleeping on the floor?"

I scratched myself through my boxer's angry bird. "We were talking about Bhaskar's love life and the girl he's sort of dating but hasn't actually talked to. Aaliya Oberoi...that's the name, Bhaskar?" He nodded, I patted my back for having pulled the I-don't-care-about-your-girl trick like a pro, and turned to the female dragon oozing fire. "DJ is on the floor because he can drink like nothing I've ever seen."

Surprisingly, Prerna was looking beyond me. I followed her gaze and landed straight on Ruchika's milky skin. She had just walked out of the bedroom. *Bhai, ab toh Prerna bohot bajayegi.*

Suddenly all the interesting aspects of my morning collided in a social train wreck.

Ruchika walked to the entrance of the kitchen, fully dressed but with messed up hair and a sleepy look on her face. *Kya mast lag rahi thi.* She paused as the three of us looked at her with dumbfounded stares.

"I was just on my way out. Umm, anyway, I had fun last night. I've left my number on your desk."

"Oh, okay," I said. "Bye."

I should have thought of something more fitting to say. But instead, I stood thinking how I would explain this to Prerna and watched her walk out the door. When the door closed, I turned to walk to the bathroom, pretending not to have noticed that Prerna was looking at me with raised eyebrows.

"Turned your alarm off?"

"Maybe it wasn't the alarm," I said.

"I was waiting for you while you were here having sex with some stranger."

I stopped and turned to face her, rolling my head to show my exasperation. "She's not a stranger. That was Ruchika."

"Ruchika what?" she asked.

"Ruchika…Jagtapar."

"You just made that up."

I put both hands on top of my head with interlocked fingers.

"No, I didn't, *meri maa*. Ruchika Jagtapar. That was her name." I dropped my hands and turned to the bathroom again. "Look, whatever. I'm going to take a shower. You guys can just hang out if you want."

Bhaskar walked back to the couch while Prerna glared at me.

"Okay, look, we didn't sleep together," I said. "I mean, we slept together but it was just sleep. Nothing happened." I followed rule no 3 religiously.

Prerna walked over to me so Bhaskar couldn't hear. "Why did you lie to me?" Even though her face was a mix of anger and hurt, she managed to be incredibly attractive. I admit that she could turn me on at least thrice a year. I usually considered her nothing more than the friend I'd had since we met in first year of college. But every once in a while, when I didn't expect it, I would notice that she was the hot girl who made most other guys stop and stare. I had never seen her have an affair, though. Weird.

She stood close enough for me to smell the strong perfume that intensified her gaze. It smelled like a strong male perfume, but that didn't matter. She was one of those girls who could pull off really short hair because her face could make a guy drop his lunch tray in the cafeteria. I took special notice of her eyes that were grey enough to make a guy forget everything and be lost in them.

"You would have gotten mad," I said as I felt a slight movement in my angry bird boxers.

She reached out and slapped me hard on my stomach.

"*Oh bhench...*, what's wrong with you?"

She walked into the living room. "I'm not mad now."

I rubbed my stomach and watched her go. I opened my mouth to say something, but stopped midway.

It was better to remain quiet. I did the only thing I could do in that situation. I turned and walked towards the bathroom. The sound of the flipping channels on the television in the living room made me think they would keep themselves occupied for a little while. I turned on the water in the shower, took off my boxers, and stepped in. The shower stream felt like a little massage, washing off the layer of party grime that coated my body after a long night of drinking. I let the water hit me on top of the head and drip over my body, slowly warming me into complete comfort.

Sundays normally called for long showers, but because Prerna and Bhaskar were in the living room with nothing to do but wait for me, I figured I'd move it along. So I pushed the soap methodically around my body, hitting all the major parts. Over my chest first, then down my arms, back up to my shoulders and neck – rinse. Then I went over the top of my back, skipped down around my butt and then came around to the front. I decided to stay there for a minute. There was a reason there was an angry bird on the front of my boxers, after all. Sure I had friends waiting for me in the living room, but they were also the friends that caused Ruchika to leave.

I decided that area needed a little extra cleaning to relieve some built-up tension. I daydreamed about all the girls I knew and many I didn't but wanted to know better – hot Sanya from last year's statistics class; sexy Manpreet from Chandigarh who I met in my bedroom on her trips to Delhi; and last but not the least, the English teacher who I knew nothing about except that I would always see her...well, you could probably figure out where I saw her.

I thought about waking up with Ruchika and imagined to be with her in her apartment. I would have to call her later. I made a quick mental note. I thought of what it would be like if she were in the shower with me.

Suddenly, I heard a knock on the door and my daydream ended instantly.

"Ronnie, I am leaving," Prerna said.

"Okay, bye," I said.

Once again, I would have liked to have said more, but in this situation, I think my restraint was justified. I'm sure she didn't understand.

I think she paused for a second, probably waiting for me to say something else and then left. I decided to forego my previous activity, finished my shower, and got out of there.

When I came out all dressed, DJ was up sipping the remains of the beer in the pitcher and Bhaskar was lying on the couch watching T.V.

I looked over at DJ. "How are you feeling?"

"Great man."

"That's what I like to hear after a night full of booze."

DJ was always cheerful in the mornings, even after having many pitchers on the previous night. I think he had requested God to give him thirty-two livers instead of thirty-two teeth. I, however, had not yet made it to that level of college partying. I knew that if I worked hard and maintained my focus, I too could reach the pinnacle of drinking.

I looked questioningly at Bhaskar.

"What?" Bhaskar asked. "Why are you looking at me like that?"

"Did she say anything about me before she left?"

"Who… Ruchika?" Bhaskar looked confused.

"No, Prerna."

"Not much. She was bitching about how you don't care about being on time and that you have a bad attitude. I don't know, she's always complaining about something. *Bahot chey chey karti hai bhai.*"

"I guess I should have met her for lunch."

"It doesn't matter," he said.

Bhaskar said it didn't matter, but he would have been there. He would have been ten minutes early, made gentlemanly conversation and been genuinely interested in what she had to say. She, in turn, would have smiled and talked about simple things. Later, she would have told her friends that she had a very pleasant time, but only if asked.

Bhaskar was the kind of guy that girls always *said* they wanted.

I was the kind of guy that they *actually* wanted.

Bhaskar was the guy girls had a pleasant time with.

I was the guy that they had an interesting time with, for better or for worse.

He thought he was doing everything right. And for the most part, he *was* doing everything right.

But where the rubber meets the road, girls don't want a guy who does everything right. It is a guy's job to rebel, at least at this age, and it's the girl's job to rebel by dating guys like me and DJ who are doing the rebelling. Bhaskar didn't get it and would never get it because he was one of the last true nice guys. That's also why he would never get Aaliya Oberoi. Funny how I could remember her name, but not the name of the girl I'd slept with the night before. Ruchika something.

On Monday morning, I woke up late. I hopped up, threw on my jeans, brushed my teeth, in short, did things supposedly necessary when rushing to college. Corners cut included showering, putting on underwear, and eating anything (other than swallowing mint-flavoured toothpaste).

I got ready for class and ran across the campus. I entered my 'Organization and Management Theory' class, one minute before it was about to start. This subject was usually called O.H.T. rather than O.M.T. as it was a complete Overhead Transmission. *By God ki kasam, kisi key baap ko samajh nahi aata tha.*

Everyone else in the class was already there. I went to the back corner of the room where I always sat, but some girl had already taken my seat. I couldn't believe it. Didn't she know it was my seat? Everybody knew where everybody was supposed to sit. Sure, there were no assigned seats, but that didn't matter. The fact was, it was my goddamn seat and somebody else was in it. *Agar Chandigarh hota toh kisi ki majaal nahi hoti bhai ki seat par baithney ki.*

"Is something wrong?" she asked, looking up at me. I realized I had been standing there for several seconds looking down at her, trying to grasp the complexity of the situation.

"No," I said. *Bas tera gala dabana hai* .

The only reason I said that was because I suddenly sensed the entire class look back at me when they heard a girl's voice. *Apney kaam sey kaam nahi rakh saktey yeh log.*

I spotted the only vacant seat in class. Three rows over in the middle. I walked and plopped myself in the seat. No sooner did I sit down that old Professor Sharma came strolling in the room.

Professor Sharma put his stuff down on the desk while everybody opened their notebooks and found their pens. I took my backpack off the top of the desk and put it beside my seat. As I bent over I saw legs, the best legs I had ever seen, I mean – perfect legs. There was a totally unbelievable set of legs in front of my face, belonging to the girl sitting at the desk next to me. Obviously, it took me a little longer than usual to reach for the right register in my backpack.

She was wearing black leather boots with good three-inch heels. I followed the legs up to the knee and around to the thigh, which curved gently to her hip and disappeared under a black skirt.

I sat back up, my register in hand, and quickly scanned her face. She was looking down at her own register, pretending not to notice that I was checking her out, but she noticed. *Ladkiyon ko sab pata hota hai ki kaun unhe dekh raha hai.* Of course she noticed. Girls who dress like that want other people to notice, and they notice when they're being noticed. What the hell am I saying? Anyway, I peeked again quickly and that's when it hit me. I recognized her face. She was wearing a little make-up, but she was none other than Aaliya Oberoi. I was dumbfounded. I guess she had been in my class all along. It occurred to me that sitting in the back corner all the time wasn't always such a great idea. It was fate. I mean, I typically don't believe in stuff like fate, but *iss baar toh vishwas karna banta tha yaar,* come on!

I thought of Bhaskar. A wave of guilt came over me. It didn't seem right to be thrilled about Aaliya being in my class. After all, I couldn't strike up a conversation with her. I couldn't allow my instincts to take over. I'd have to fight the urge to try to start some kind of relationship with her. I would just have to let it go and let her be Bhaskar's dream girl. In the next class, I would just go back to my little seat in the corner and forget this encounter.

At that very moment, Aaliya Oberoi dropped her pen. As if in slow motion, it slipped out of her hand and tumbled to the floor, bouncing slightly before coming to rest a few inches from my left foot. She might as well have just turned to me, told me she loved me, and invited me over to her place. *Please yaar, jaisey ki mujhe pata hee nahin ki casually pen giraaney ka kya matlab hai.*

And there it was, the pen, sitting at my feet like an etched invitation. I reached down to pick it up for her like a gentleman. *Farz banta tha yaar mera. Chandigarh ki izzat ka sawaal tha.*

"Here you go."

"Oh, thanks," she said. She smiled as she tossed her hair over to one side and reached for the pen.

There wasn't much I could make sense of in Prof. Sharma's words, and thanked my stars when the class finally ended. I thought about saying something to Aaliya. After all, we had shared that bond with the pen and everything, so it wouldn't be too odd. But I couldn't think of anything clever to say, so I let her go. She walked out of the room with her long hair bopping behind her. I followed her, leaving enough distance between us that it didn't look like I was following her, but not so much distance that I couldn't get a decent look.

Thoughts quickly drifted from Aaliya to Bhaskar, and Bhaskar to the morning conversation, and finally to Prerna. I had promised to meet her for lunch in the cafeteria.

> **Rule 4: Don't make promises. If you do, you can only break them once. Breaking a promise with the same person twice can be really dangerous. Avoid it.**

Every day, Prerna and I went to grab lunch, and every day I hoped and prayed and promised myself that I would find something to eat other than a bowl of coloured water which was sometimes called *daal*, sometimes *kadi* and sometimes *rajma*. But all that changed was the colour of the water. The taste was the same – like sea water. Hats off to consistency! *Abhi Chandigarh mein hota toh mast desi ghee mein banaa tasty khana hota.*

I bumped into her on the way to the cafeteria. We walked through the main hall, full of students sitting together but socializing on Facebook on their phones. We took our food and Prerna led the way to a table in the middle of the cafeteria.

Prerna and I sat in silence for a few seconds. I was checking out what was there in the coloured water bowl today when she suddenly spoke up.

"Oh, she's hot," she said.

"Who?" I asked calmly.

"Right there. See her?'

The girl was hot, but that wasn't the point.

"The one in the red top?"

"No. The curly hair girl in the black denims."

"Her? I can't see her face."

"Trust me she's..."

"Oh, wait. I see her. You think she's hot? Really? But why are you checking out girls? That is supposed to be my job."

I knew where she was getting at. If I praised that girl, she would show how jealous she is and hint at her attraction towards me. And getting me to admit her attraction would be a huge triumph.

"No, I don't think she is hot. Just look at her breasts!" *Did I just say that? Lag gayi beta, gyan session shuru hoga ab mata ji ka.*

Prerna glanced at the girl and looked back at me. "You are a pig. All you see in a girl is her breasts."

Well, *ab jo sach hai who sach hai.* But I couldn't debate the same with her so I took a bite of my *roti* and dipped it in the yellow *daal* water for some time and popped it into my mouth. Actually even Prerna had great breasts. As I looked at Prerna, I realized how much I wanted to impress her, and how many times I'd tried, and how I never really could.

I wondered why nobody could impress her.

"What?" she asked. "What are you looking at?"

"Nothing," I said.

Thankfully she changed the topic. "How is Ruchika?" Prerna asked.

"Oh god, not again. You're fascinated with that girl."

"I just asked because she's right over there," she said.

I turned my head to look in the direction that Prerna was looking and, there she was – Ruchika something. *Fuck, what was her last name?* I knew I wasn't going to talk to her and that she wasn't going to talk to me, but I knew Prerna wanted to shake things up.

I held my ground and turned back toward her calmly. "So?"

"Go talk to her. Come on, she probably misses you," she grinned with her devilish smile.

Just then, out of the blue, Bhaskar came and sat down beside me. For the first time in my life, I was so happy to see Bhaskar. He had just saved me from an awkward situation.

"Hey guys! What's up?" he asked.

"Ronnie was just going to talk to his true love," said Prerna.

But Bhaskar had his own story waiting to pop out of his mouth. "What! Wait, you're not going to believe this. Guess who's in my social class?"

"Who?" I asked.

"That girl Ruchika, who was at your house."

"That's perfect!" said Prerna. "Now you have to go talk to her. Hey Bhaskar, is her last name Jagtapar?"

"I don't know."

"Find out for me," Prerna said.

"*Ab bas bhi kar yaar,*" I said.

At that point I decided not to tell Bhaskar that Aaliya Oberoi was in my OHT class. I decided to wait for a better moment. This was not the moment.

"Just admit that you don't know her last name," Prerna said.

"Okay, I don't know."

"See, you really *are* a pig."

"How does that make me a pig?"

"Bhaskar, do you like a girl because of her breasts?" Prerna asked.

"I don't know. Is there a right answer to this?" Bhaskar seemed perplexed.

"According to her there is," I said.

"Well, then yes, 'breasts' is the answer," Bhaskar said innocently.

"You're a pig too," Prerna said.

Bhaskar looked really hurt.

I was getting tired of her. *Bahot pakaa rahi thi.*

She should understand that breasts were the main reason that boys had difficulty in making eye contact with girls. I think Prerna was too influenced by Bollywood movies. Though she was really modern and all, but she loved Zeenat Amaan. I remembered the scene from *Qurbaani* movie which I saw at Prerna's place where Zeenat Amaan was standing in a bikini singing: "*Kya dekhtey ho*" and Feroz Khan sang back "*Soorat tumhari*". I am sure he was not looking at her face. I think I have made my point.

The next afternoon crawled on at glacial pace. I sat in my apartment for a few minutes, decompressing, listening to Sri Sri Honey Singh, thinking of nothing. The late-afternoon sun streamed through the window and lit swirling particles floating in the air. Something about it made me feel like I lived inside a giant nostril. There were clusters of stuff everywhere – photographs on the table, piles of CDs on the floor, take-out menus on the countertop. One cabinet was open, and I could see an old package of green tea beckoning me. Tea, why not? Antioxidants might come in handy.

I opened the refrigerator and took out the bottle on the top shelf. It was empty. I placed it back. I filled the pan with tap water and boiled the water, while I washed a mug. I had no sugar so I poured a few drops of mojitos cocktail syrup in it. I took a sip. It tasted great. I opened my window and then sat blowing on the tea.

Bhaskar came over after his afternoon class to hang out. We played online *teen patti* where Bhaskar lost many e-rupees and I wished I had played the real game. He was sad and I was having a good time. I thought it was a great time to break the news about Aaliya being in my class.

"Bhaskar, I got something to tell you. But I want you to relax and listen calmly," I said.

"What is it?"

"Aaliya Oberoi is in my OHT class."

"What? *Kya baat kar raha hai Ronnie bhai, abhi tak bataya kyu nahi?*"

"*Bataa toh raha hun ab,*" I said. I always thought that was good response when somebody asked why I didn't tell them something.

"*Chal woh sab chhor mere bhai. Kuch setting karaa dey yaar.* You are really good at this stuff," he said.

I was really good at this stuff, I knew, but I had a hunch Aaliya was equally good. She would know that I am setting her up. And Bhaskar was not good at this stuff.

Bhaskar looked at me with those eager eyes and I knew if I said, 'It will never work,' he would counter with something like, 'I know it will work bro, let's just try it.'

"Bhaskar, it will never work," I said.

"I know it will work bro, let's just try it," he said.

I almost hate being right all the time.

"Alright," I said. "But if it doesn't work, then it's over. I can get you one chance with her. That's all."

"*Bilkul Bhai. Bas tu plan bataa mere bhai,*" he said. "If you plan it, it'll definitely work."

"Just meet me when the class ends and I will get you introduced."

"Okay, I'll be there."

The next day, I came to class early because I wanted to grab the seat next to Aaliya. She wasn't there yet. I was waiting, fiddling with my iPhone, when I noticed a girl standing beside me.

"You're in my seat," she said.

I looked up at her. I had no idea who she was, but she was gorgeous. I find most girls gorgeous, yes, but she really was.

"You're in my seat," she said again. "I sit here every class. It's my seat."

"I sat here last class," I said.

"I was not well that day."

"Well, the seats are not assigned and I can sit anywhere I like," I casually responded.

"That doesn't matter. We always sit in the same seats anyway."

"Who made that rule? I have never heard of it. I'm sitting here today," I said.

"Seriously, you want to fight over a seat."

"Exactly my point." I grinned confidently.

She sat down in front of me, hitting the table and moving the chair making as much noise as possible to express her anger.

I thought everyone was looking at me. But it didn't matter. I was on a mission *yaar*.

Aaliya Oberoi marched into the room in another stunning outfit. Denim skirt, boots and a hooded sweatshirt. Okay, it wasn't so much the clothes as the way she wore them, or the way she walked, or the way she… *oh pata nahi yaar*, she just looked good.

She sat down beside me without looking at me.

I took a moment to think of a good opening line. It had to be stylish yet manly, unintended with a hint of romance, inviting but playful, confident with a touch of humour. What would the ideal statement that draws her into my very soul and cause her to fall victim to my charms? After much deliberation and thinking I knew what I had to say.

"Hey, what's up?" I asked.

"Oh, hi," she said.

I cracked it.

"Have you been reading all these books?" I asked pointing to the books she had placed on the table. *Ab kuchh toh puchna tha mujhe.*

"Oh god, no," she said laughing. "I haven't even opened them yet. I'm going to inaugurate them before the test."

"What test? When?" I asked.

"Next Tuesday, isn't it?"

"Oh yeah," I said although I had no clue that there was an OHT test. I had spent the last class with her legs, after all.

By God ki kasam, meri toh lag gayi. I would fail miserably.

All of a sudden, my life was much more complicated. There was a test next week, Bhaskar's love life after class, and Aaliya's legs right beside me. What was I going to do? I opted for the last.

"My name's Ronnie by the way," I said.

"I'm Aaliya."

"Do you think you'll be ready for this test?"

"Yeah, I guess. I'll have to do a lot of studying this week. How about you?" she asked.

"I don't know. I hope so. Though I have attended most of the classes but I will have to do lot of cramming myself."

"You've been to every class? I've never seen you before the last class," she said.

"I used to sit in the corner," I said.

"But why did you move to this seat?"

"Yes, why did you move?" the girl in front of me chimed in.

"I needed some change in my life." I said turning to smile at the seat-snatcher girl. She didn't smile back.

"We all need a change sometimes," Aaliya said.

How deep. The words trickled like poetry from her ravishing lips. But the moment was spoiled when Prof. Sharma walked into the room and moved his lips.

He didn't waste any time starting his boring lecture, babbling about the stuff I was supposed to be listening to. But how was I supposed to listen when I had Aaliya, who was clearly interested in continuing our fascinating discussion, sitting next to me. The rest of the class was uninteresting except for those holy moments when Aaliya uncrossed and re-crossed her legs. Eight times.

"Oh God this was a never ending class," I said to Aaliya.
"Yeah, tell me about it!" she said.

Bilkul mere type ki ladki thi yaar. She gathered her books and readied herself to walk out the door. I was sure to take the same amount of time that she did in order to gather my things. I opportunely lined up beside her in order to strike up some more conversation.

"I had an idea," I said.

She looked over at me, slightly alarmed, slightly interested. I continued anyway. *Kuch toh bolna tha yaar.*

"What would you think about getting together and studying for the test sometime?" I asked.

"I don't know, I usually . . ."

"I usually don't study with anyone either. I mean, we'll study the stuff on our own, but like, get together and quiz each other," I said.

We were almost out the door when I realized the huge mistake I had just made. I was supposed to make small talk with her, not make a date. How was I going to explain that one to Bhaskar?

"Okay. That sounds good," she said.

I wanted to take it all back, but it was too late. And speaking of too late, there was Bhaskar, standing against the wall as the crowd of people pushed passed him.

"Ronnie!" he called, like I couldn't see him. "What's up?"

"Hey, man," I said.

He fought his way through the crowd in order to get next to me and Aaliya. He was making it so obvious. *Marwayega yeh pakka mujhe.*

"Where are you going?" he asked.

"I just got out of class. I'm heading back to my apartment."

I hated the made-up chat already. I turned my attention back to Aaliya.

"So Aaliya, if you give me your number I can call you and we'll set something up."

"Sure, whatever. Let's get outside and I will message you my number," she said.

I saw my chance for the big introduction.

"Bhaskar, this is Aaliya. Aaliya, Bhaskar."

"Hi, it's nice to meet you," he said.

"Nice to meet you, too," she said.

How fake. How stupid. She would have surely smelled the set-up. Girls like her had lived through so many set-ups that they knew what was going on. *Ab pogo channel dekh kar badi thodi hui hogi woh.* Hell, she probably knew what I was going to say before I did.

We got out of the building and I felt the relief of the air touching my face. Aaliya started digging in her bag to find her mobile.

I was happy that she couldn't find her phone as that would give Bhaskar some time to say something meaningful to her.

I waited and waited; Bhaskar stood staring; Aaliya fiddled in her bag. And he stared. And she fiddled.

And I stood. And he stared. And she fiddled.

Is dhakkan sey kuch nahi hoga. "Bhaskar, what are you doing for lunch?" I asked.

"I don't know. Cafeteria, I guess."

"I think I am, too. Aaliya, you want to join us?"

She found her phone and asked me my number. While she gave me a buzz, she said, "Sorry, I'm meeting someone, but thanks anyway."

Actually what she meant to say was: "Fuck off guys. I know what you are trying to do. *Main shikarpur sey nahin aayi hoon.*"

"Did you get my missed call?" she said.

I smiled as the eternal light blinked in my iPhone. "Yes I got it."

Bhaskar watched the number blink in my phone.

"Thanks. I'll call you," I said. What I meant to say was: "I really need you, you are so hot."

"Okay, bye. It was nice meeting you Bhaskar," she said.

"It was nice meeting you, too," said Bhaskar and blushed. Almost.

And she walked. Bhaskar stared. And she walked.

"Man, that was great! You even got her number," Bhaskar said.

What Bhaskar didn't seem to understand was that *I* got her number; he didn't.

"*Saaley, teri phatt kyun gayi?* You were supposed to invite her to lunch. You know, talk to her more," I said.

"I didn't need to. You invited her. And she said no anyway."

"That's not the point. You were just supposed to talk to her and get to know her a little bit so you could see her on campus and talk to her more."

"I did that. I'll talk to her when I see her again," he said.

I wondered if she would talk to him the way she spoke to me. Guilt was washed over by temptation.

Rule 5: Never use a friend to hook you up with the person you like. Your friend might just betray you.

He thought his meeting with Aaliya was a great success, and I decided to let him feel happy?

Yeah, I knew how Bhaskar's relationship would end up with her. But my relationship with her on the other hand… well, I had no idea how that would turn out. I would call her, she would come over. That part I could probably bet on. We would study, which was a joke in itself, and who knows what would happen from there. I don't even know how I managed to make a date with her.

Okay, it wasn't really a date. She probably didn't think it was a date. But in college, studying didn't really mean studying and everyone knew that. Except for Bhaskar.

"So maybe when she comes over to your place to study, I could be there and talk to her more," Bhaskar said.

"Well, maybe. Or maybe I could just give you her phone number and you could call her."

"I don't know. I don't think she'd want to talk to me. Maybe I could wait outside your class again on Friday," he said.

"Bhaskar, this can't go on forever." *Chaep kyun ho raha hai.*

"Not forever. Maybe just Friday. Then she'd be used to me and I could call her," he said.

Aaliya isi ka toh intezaar kar rahi thi sadiyon sey . That was probably it. She was just waiting for him to whisk her away from her dull world of popularity. But there wasn't much hope in trying to explain all that to Bhaskar. He had such a glow in his eyes when he talked about her that I just couldn't bring myself to dash his hopes of romance.

No, I wouldn't do anything more to crush Bhaskar's dreams. But there was one thing I could do for myself – happy hours night at the Matchbox lounge.

For the rest of the day – through classes, mealtimes, and all social interactions – my mind was focused on that one, central goal. And who better to share in it with than the grand master of the ceremony himself: DJ.

DJ had perfected the art of happy hour night. I think when he was in school and his teacher would have asked him: Beta DJ, what is 1+1?

DJ would have replied: Ma'am, happy hour.

At seven o'clock we got ready to move out. The beer went back to the regular price at 10 p.m., so we had to get going. DJ got ready by walking out to the living room and saying, "Let's go." And I got ready by rolling off the couch and springing into an upright position, quite athletically I might add. We weren't much for dressing up.

Close proximity is a good feature for a bar when you're in a drunken lethargy so we always chose Matchbox, which wasn't

far away. The historic Hauz Khas village was the funkiest spot in south Delhi to shop, eat, party or to just generally enjoy the vibe.

As we entered the lounge, the smell of beer welcomed us in. It felt like coming home. It was a dimly lit place, few couches–all occupied, few high stools–all occupied, a bar–completely occupied. Getting a beer was no easy task, but it wouldn't be a problem for DJ. I had seen him get beer at bars more crowded than this.

"I'm going for the bar," DJ said.

Even Prerna with her good looks and "I don't care a fuck about you guys" attitude could push through the guys and get a beer. All three of us had perfected this art.

I spotted Prerna across the bar, talking to some hot girls. I allowed myself the momentary erotic dream of having a three-some with them. I had never had a threesome, but it sounded like something for the memoir. Although it was probably a little nerve-racking. There were a lot of holes and things that a guy needed to tend to in a situation like that, a lot of sexual multitasking. You had to play your best game.

I gave Prerna about ten minutes before she saw me, ditched the girls, and came over. *Yeh toh hona hee tha.*

After a couple of minutes, DJ came back through the crowd, two beers in hand.

"Here you go, dude. You get the next round," he said.

"That was fast. Might be a new record for you," I said.

"No way. I got four beers in a minute last time."

The cold beer hit my lips and slid down as if an ice cube had slip down a volcano. *Aaahaa.*

"What are you guys doing?" Prerna asked.

I turned to see Prerna looking at me.

"Hey, not much," I said. "What are you up to? Who are those girls you're with?"

"Some girl invited me here and those are her friends."

"Whatever," DJ said. "Hey Ronnie, I'll see you in a little bit." I turned back toward Prerna as DJ walked away.

"Why do you hang out with him?" she asked.

"I don't know. I'm still trying to figure out why I hang out with you."

"Because you want me."

"Oh, thanks for clearing that up," I said.

"So what did you do today?"

"Tried to get Bhaskar his dream girl. You know, usual stuff," I said.

"I'm sick of hearing about her already. Let me call her and put an end to this," she said.

I certainly wasn't going to give her Aaliya's number because I knew she wasn't kidding. Given the chance, Prerna would actually call Aaliya.

She would probably end up threatening her or something. My impression was that Aaliya wasn't all that different from Prerna in some ways, and I wouldn't be surprised if they got into a fight.

I imagined how hot this fight would be. Two hot girls fighting each other, tearing each other's clothes, just so that the winner could have me. I was so interested in what a fight between those two would look like that I momentarily considered giving Aaliya's number to Prerna.

"I don't think you should call her," I said.

"Why? Are you afraid of what I'd say?" asked Prerna.

Was she serious?

"No," I said. "I just think Bhaskar needs to work this out for himself. He might get hurt, but he'll learn from it and be a better person because of it. He'll grow from the experience."

I sounded like Ramdev Baba giving a *pravachan* on love life.

"Whatever," Prerna said, taking a swig of her beer.

Just then, I got a slap on the back.

"Ronnie! Hi, I haven't seen you in so long!"

I turned around to see an attractive girl looking very excited to see me. I knew her, but I had no idea where I knew her from. She had been in one of my classes, or was a friend of a friend or something. But what was her name? Preeti? Shruti? Something like that.

"Hey, what's going on? What have you been up to?" I said, forcing myself to sound excited.

"Not much. It's so funny. I thought about you today out of the blue. I was wondering what happened to you. And then, here you are," she said.

"Here I am!"

"I'd like you to meet Prerna," I said. This of course was a clever tactic to find out her name.

"Hi, I'm Aditi," she said.

At least I got the rhyming correct – Preeti, Shruti, Aditi!

"Hi, it's nice to meet you," Prerna said. They shook hands and were quite pleasant. But somehow it always felt a little odd to introduce people to Prerna. They probably thought they were meeting a girl who was popular, fun, and maybe slightly stuck on herself. A girl that all the girls wanted to be friends with and all the guys wanted to sleep with. But she was none of those.

After they shook hands, they both looked at me, waiting for me to do some ice breaking for the two strangers meeting for the first time. What I wanted to say was, 'Okay, let's do a three-some.'

But that wouldn't have been appropriate.

"So, how long have you been here?" I asked.

"About six mugs," Aditi laughed.

Come to think of it, it brings me rule no 6.

Rule 6: When you happen to meet you 'EX' in a drunken state, just leave everyone else and focus on her. Have faith in destiny and it shall lead you to her bedroom (or yours!). Of course, a few more drinks later.

Oh, she was drunk all right. And that made her much more gorgeous. Isn't that funny? Getting drunk normally makes everyone else look more attractive, but being sober when other people, especially girls are drunk, can make them more attractive, too. Maybe I could do Ph.D. and become a doctor. I could write my thesis on 'Beer and the attractiveness of a girl'.

The research in itself would be so much fun. Just imagine!

So Shruti, I mean Aditi, continued to flirt with me. We talked about the good old times we had even though I couldn't remember any of the good old times myself. Prerna got tired of listening to Aditi after a while. She knew where I was heading. She took me to a side while Aditi gulped her beer.

"Don't sleep with her, okay? I know it's none of my business, but just don't," she said.

"Why? Are you jealous?" I asked.

"Hardly! I don't care. I'm leaving. You can do whatever you want."

Prerna went back to the other girls for the rest of the night. But she kept looking over at me for the next few hours. I, of course, pretended not to notice.

Twenty minutes later, I found myself in the ladies' bathroom sharing a joint with Aditi. She had been out for a while and had the determination to prove it further. She dragged me by my hand to the ladies' room, whispering, "C'mon handsome, let's get high." I was a bit taken aback at first; she seemed the one who liked being on top. She looked damn sexy in a short bright-pink skirt and a baby pink tank top. Her nipples, like the built-in timer in my microwave were declaring, "Chicken's ready!"

Aditi handed me the joint after taking a long pull, and before I could put it to my lips she put her mouth next to mine and blew the smoke in. It was a sexy move and my Bull instantly improved his posture.

We had almost plunged into the act when someone pounded at the door, and we ignored it.

The moment was to be treasured. I had never shared a joint in this manner. It somehow started hitting me more coming from her lips. Or maybe not.

She moved in and kissed me sloppily. I made her hand trail down my stomach towards Bull and she hesitantly grabbed Bull through my pants. Instantly I was as hard as a lamppost on the streets. I slipped my hand up her skirt. What a great landscape.

There was a series of rude knocks at the door and we jerked off our intimate position.

"Not here," she said suddenly, straightening her skirt. She stubbed out the joint in the sink.

We opened the bathroom door and stepped out past a girl who glared at us.

Aditi and I headed for the door. DJ was lost somewhere in the beer pitchers and I knew he wouldn't be ready to go for quite a while anyway.

So the two of us headed outside with our bellies full of alcohol and our head full of hash. Aditi waved her hand and a cab stopped immediately. Aditi told him to drive down to Malviya Nagar which was a few minutes away.

I was feeling a bit uneasy as the cab driver managed to hit every single pot hole on the way to Aditi's apartment. Riding in the back of the cabs sometimes nauseated me. I stared outside the window and watched stores, lampposts and pavements pass.

The cab driver was zooming as if he were in a race. We traversed the next two kilometres in silence. But suddenly the cab screeched to the curb and we were there. I pulled out the money and we stood on an empty street, in front of a bungalow.

Aditi asked me to keep my volume low and we tip-toed to the gate. She opened the lock quietly so that her landlord didn't wake up and we sneaked inside the gate and walked up to a black iron spiral ladder which led to the top floor. My head was already spiralling and I wondered how I would reach the top of this spiral ladder. I followed Aditi's legs. *Karna toh tha. I was on a mission.*

"Oh my God, is this your bedroom?" I asked, stumbling in. This was a groundbreaking moment. Her bedroom was completely pink. Pink bedsheets, pink pillow covers, pink almirah. I finally checked her clothes again. Oh they were pink. I should have known. She was the girl from Lady Sriram College. I had met her in the last college festival 'Crossroads' and come to this same room and we had sneaked in the same way.

"Yeah," she said.

My mind oscillated back to Prerna. It was cute how Prerna asked me not to sleep with Aditi. She kind of looked out for me, in a caring sort of way. She was a good girl.

My thoughts turned to Aaliya. If she had been in the bedroom, well, it would just be great.

I switched off the lights and walked towards Aaliya. Oh sorry, towards Aditi.

The morning came too early, as mornings always seem to. I got off the bed and slowly made my way to the bathroom. I didn't want to wake her up. The only reason I usually got out of bed in the morning was to pee. If it weren't for that, I'd probably never leave my bed.

Can you imagine a world where you never had to go to the bathroom? You could just stay in bed all the time. Awesomeness.

After leaving the bathroom and feeling much better, I quietly slid out of her room, hopped into an autorickshaw and went to my apartment.

I reached home, got ready and went to college. I walked into economics class and found my seat in the back. Luckily, it was vacant this time. The professor walked in, set his bag down and yelled, "What is the law of diminishing marginal utility?"

Everyone was startled. Then they all lowered their heads, opened their notebooks, and pretended to look like they really cared about what marginal utility was. No one looked at him or at anyone else. I followed suit, opening my notebook so I wouldn't stand out among the class. Standing out was a sure-shot way to get called on.

The prof proudly surveyed the class. "What is the law of diminishing marginal utility?" he asked again.

One nerd raised his hand and proudly stood up. "Law of diminishing marginal utility means that the first unit of consumption of a good or service yields more utility than the second and subsequent units, with a continuing reduction for greater amounts. For example, if I drink one cup of tea, I will like it, but I won't enjoy the next cup as much as I enjoyed the first one and so on. The tenth cup would really give me no enjoyment."

"Well done," said the professor with gleaming eyes.

I thought about how much money my parents paid for me to take all these classes I didn't need. I already knew that this law of marginal utility was not true. I have one glass of beer, then I want to have another and then another. The enjoyment keeps increasing. I have many more examples to prove my logic. I sleep with one girl, I enjoy it; I sleep with another I enjoy it more and so on.

Now that's why this is a crap law of marginal fuck-tility! So as usual, I found myself wasting another hour of my life listening to the opinions of guys who were like…ten thousand years old, telling me wrong laws which had no meaning in real life.

The class finished and I walked over to the cafeteria for lunch and found Prerna waiting for me where she always waited for me. I was a little surprised. I gave it a fifty-fifty chance whether she would be there or not as she knew last night I had left her for the drunken girl Shruti, or Aditi or whatever her name was.

"Hey," she said.

"What's up?" I asked.

"Nothing. So?"

"So what?"

I loved playing that game. The one where you pretend that you don't know what the other person is talking about even though you know exactly what they're talking about just so you can make them struggle for a little longer. Hey, it's not easy being such a *kameena* and staying elusive about it.

"Did you sleep with her?" she asked.

"Isn't that a little personal?"

"Oh, like you're so shy about your sex life," she said.

"Relax, I slept on the couch."

"I don't believe you."

"Okay," I said.

"I know you slept with her."

There was really no winning with her.

We made it down the long queue, got our lunches which looked as bad as ever and found our seats without speaking to each other, yet not making it seem like we weren't speaking to each other.

"Did Bhaskar go out with that girl yet?" asked Prerna.

"Who?"

I was doing it again. *By God ki kasam, I was a true kameena.*

"That hot girl in your OHT class. What's her name?"

"Oh, Aaliya," I said. "No. It probably won't happen."

"Why?"

"You know Bhaskar."

"I know. And more importantly, I know you. And if you're the one helping him, then he'll probably never go out with her," she said.

"Whatever."

We sat in silence for a few more minutes, eating our bad lunches. I looked at her as she ate. She knew I was looking at her but she pretended to ignore me. I started thinking about the night before and how she was there with me in the bar. She could have come over to my place if I had played it right. But as usual, I was too indifferent about the whole situation.

And then it happened. I looked at her and felt a tingling below. The kind of tingling that reminds you that you're a man and that there's something you were put on earth to do. Even though the tingling hit at an unsuitable time, I kept looking at her anyway, thinking of what might have been and what still might be. I started to feel...longer.

"Are you going out tonight?" Prerna asked.

"What?"

"Are you going out tonight?"

"Uh, no. I don't think so," I said.

Why did she have to start talking? The visual accompanied with audio was even more arousing. That was just making things worse. It actually started to become longer. I was kind of enjoying the moment; just that my jeans were so restrictive.

"Hey, there's Bhaskar," Prerna said.

I looked over to see Bhaskar standing in the queue. He was waving desperately at me.

"Why don't you just go over and see what he wants?" asked Prerna.

"Because I want to eat," I said. How could I explain to her that this was not the time to get up. My bull was exploding out of my jeans.

It was amazing how fast a little anxiety could shrink an erection. I started thinking about some ugly people and some horror movies. I needed help to ensure that the candidate didn't keep standing up against me. Within a few short seconds, I was ready to be on the move.

"Okay, alright. I'll see what he wants," I said.

I got up from the table and walked over to Bhaskar.

"Hey Bhaskar, what's up?" I asked.

"Did you call her?"

"Call who?" I was doing it again. *Kameenepan ka naya record!*

"Aaliya," he said.

"No. I'll probably see her in class tomorrow and talk to her then."

"Come on! She gave you her phone number. You should call her," he said.

Bas ab yahi rah gaya tha life mein. Of all the people in the world, Bhaskar was giving me advice.

"Relax, I'll talk to her tomorrow," I said.

"You know, I've been thinking about it. Maybe I should call her," he said.

"Why?"

"Because then she could get to know me better and I could ask her out."

"Hmm. Not such a good idea," I said.

The truth is, if Bhaskar was going to go out with her, the last thing he should want is for her to get to know him better. He should talk to her just a little and then ask her out. Then they would go on one date and one date only. It would be a date that had been played out a hundred times throughout history. Ever since the concept of dating was invented, Bhaskar would add to the history of "DON'T's" in the dating history book.

"We can talk about this in a few minutes," I said to Bhaskar. "Just get your food and sit down. We're over there."

I walked back over to Prerna and sat down.

"What did he want?" she said.

"Nothing."

"Fine," she said. It was the same tone of "fine" that had landed many a man in a pool of trouble.

Prerna always thought I was keeping stuff from her. She was one of those people who thought that NASA had found life on Mars but they covered it up and didn't tell anyone. In her mind, if NASA was trying to keep stuff like that from her, I was definitely going to keep whatever Bhaskar said to me from her.

"He just wanted to know if I called that girl yet," I said.

"He wants you to call her for him? Doesn't he know he is not a kid anymore? He has got to do his thing."

"Don't give him a hard time about it. He thinks this will be the best way. I'm kind of a buffer for his feelings, I think. *Samjha kar yaar,* I am the one who has to get him his *pyaar.*"

"You boys do what you want," she said, trying to sound unconcerned, but I knew better than that.

Just about then, Bhaskar came over. Prerna started off on him even before he could settle down on the table.

"Why do you want Ronnie to call some girl for you? Girls don't like that. You have to show some confidence if you think you're going to go out with her," she said.

"What do you know?" asked Bhaskar.

Oh beta! A splitting comeback. I had to step in and give him some help.

"Yeah, Prerna. Do you think you could pick up a girl if you were a guy? Do you think it would be that easy?" I asked.

"Hell yeah. I know what girls like," she said.

How annoying. What she said actually made sense.

Anyway, Prerna left Bhaskar alone after that because she had made her point, and Bhaskar left Prerna alone because he was scared of her. I left both of them alone because I knew it was of no use.

And then came Friday, my reason for living in this world. I think that for everything bad in this world, there has to be something good to counter-balance it. God created Monday, therefore, he also created Friday. See how it works? Today was when I would again get a chance to sit next to Aaliya.

I walked down to my class and noted that there weren't many people around. I was a little late as usual. I strolled into class, but didn't run to take *the* seat. I didn't want to look like a *chutiya*. *By God ki kasam, apna bhi kuch style tha bhai.*

I saw that the *seat chor* had already taken the seat next to Aaliya. She was looking towards me with a devilish smile, flashing all her teeth. What a bitch! *Abhi Chandigarh hota toh seat sey utha deta isko. Ainvyi bond ban rahi hai. Do pyaar karne walon ko juda kar diya.*

I needed the new seat beside Aaliya if I were to win her over with my charms. Suddenly, Professor Sharma came to the door. There was no time left. I had to make a move. There was only one seat that wasn't taken, and it was in the front row. *Bencho lag gayi! First seat par toh chutiye baithtey hain. Aaliya kya sochegi mere baarey mein.*

Oh bencho! There was no one in front of me. Never before had I experienced anything like that – no buffer between me and the teacher – no one to hide behind, look at, or space out. I could be called on at any moment. How dreadful! I felt like a gladiator sent to a war without his armour and shield.

I pulled out my notebook and pen and prepared to write. I would actually have to take notes. Could I do it? Was I ready for that kind of responsibility?

"What do you say we continue where we left last time?" Prof. Sharma asked.

I hated when teachers asked the class if it would be okay to proceed. I was tempted to raise my hand and say, "No, it wouldn't be okay to continue. We want to go out and watch a movie instead. *Aaya badaa.*"

"What's your name?" Sharma asked.

It was happening already. I couldn't believe it.

"Ronnie," I said.

"Ronnie, can you tell us where we left at the class?"

I had no fucking clue what he was asking.

I sheepishly looked at him.

He was killing me. I felt Aaliya's eyes looking at me, witnessing this whole incident.

She was thinking I was a total *chutiya* and there was no way she would study with me.

Someone behind me blabbered out the answer in one go.

How unbelievably irritating! Some jerk had just made me look worse. I was dying to glance back and see who it was. *Ek number key chutiye bharey padey they class mein.* I paused for a second and then with a quick jerk of the head, I turned to see who it was. In the same instant, I turned back to the window. It was the *seat-chor* girl. I knew it. I looked forward again. I noticed Aaliya had glanced at me while I was glancing at the *seat-chor*. All the glancing was driving me crazy. I hated the front row.

When the class ended, I threw my stuff in my backpack slowly and purposefully, carefully planning to stand up just a few seconds after Aaliya so we would be walking out together. I made my little glances toward her to time it just right.

"Hi," she said as we walked out together.

"Hey, how's it going?" I acted surprised, like I hadn't noticed she was there.

Rule 7: If you want to be with someone, don't just go like a fool and open your heart out. Just act casual. That would make you more appealing and she would want you more than ever.

"Pretty good," she said.

We walked out into the hall where I saw Bhaskar standing against the wall a few classrooms down. I really didn't want to see him.

"Did you know what Prof. Sharma was asking about?" I asked Aaliya.

"No!" she said opening her big eyes wider. "I felt so bad for you. I was glad he didn't call on me. I haven't studied much. I totally have to do it this weekend. Do you still want to study?"

"Yeah, sure," I said.

But suddenly I wasn't so sure. She didn't know anything about the subject either. I thought she was going to help me in this subject. *But bhai isko toh khud kuch nahi aata tha.* I was on my way to failing the test and I was going to get help from someone as incompetent as I was.

"Ronnie. What's up?" Bhaskar asked.

"Oh, hey, Bhaskar. Not much. What are you doing?"

"Nothing. Do you want to go to lunch?" he asked.

"Yes, sure," I said.

"I'll talk to you later," Aaliya said. She was off down the corridor and disappeared into the sea of humanity. When she was out of sight, Bhaskar turned toward me.

"What was that?" he asked.

"What was what?"

"That. She just walked away," he said.

"I can't help it. She can do whatever she wants," I said.

Bhaskar was losing it.

I didn't want to look like a fool on my study date with Aaliya so I thought of studying the subject beforehand. With a hand on my heart I took the most difficult decision of my life. It was tough, but I summed up the courage for it. Yes, I was going to go the library. *By God ki kasam ladki pataaney ke liye bahot kuch karna padta hai bhai.*

I wondered how the library would look like. I asked for directions, and it seemed like a game of treasure hunt, everyone was giving different clues. I think not many of my friends knew about the location of the library. I even checked on the maps on my iPhone. No luck.

So I wandered around asking people and finally a nerdy guy helped me out. I walked a few metres and reached the destination. The library was a huge concrete building in the middle of the campus. The whole building was quite a piece of architecture, I'll have to admit. It had big pillars, a large board in front and huge glass windows.

I entered the library and looked ahead. A divine light was flashing in front of my eyes. I could hear bells ringing, those large golden bells in a Hindu temple. It was like Amitabh Bachchan had come to the temple for the first time in the movie *Nastik*. Today I could understand how he must have felt. I wanted to say: "*Main agaya hoon maa, haiiiin.*"

There was a large study area on the first floor with a bunch of big tables where people could study together and were allowed to talk at hush levels.

I got to the study area and pushed myself down in a chair which was near the windows. I opened my book and the brand new binding cracked. I flipped the crisp pages until I got to chapter four. I started to read about the unbelievably boring world of the obvious. After an hour, I found myself waking up. No, I hadn't slept the whole one hour. I read a good two pages before I dozed off.

I wiped the saliva off the third page of chapter four. I glanced around quickly to see if anyone had noticed. Most of them were either deep into studying, talking to someone, or sleeping themselves. I wiped the corner of my mouth and put my hand over my forehead and leaned my elbow on the desk, acting like I was reading.

I moved along with the reading, soaking up decades of scholarly knowledge. That's when I heard someone sitting down at my table a few chairs away. I could tell it was a girl without looking, just by the sounds she made as she sat down and got out her books. Oh, and let's not forget that great smell that skilfully made its way and managed to send me to a better place.

For some reason I could sense she was attractive. I had to look. Nothing could stop it. I glanced over just as she turned away and leaned down to set her back pack beside the desk. I looked back at my book again as she sat up. She had a nice figure. I could tell that from the little I saw. But I hadn't seen her face, so I had to look again. I looked over and took in as much of her face as I could in a quick glance.

She was attractive, but more importantly, familiar. I found myself looking back again only to find her looking at me. Some days I just couldn't win. It was the *seat-chor*.

"Hi," she said. "Aren't you in my OHT class?"

Surely that was a rhetorical question.

"Yeah," I said.

"Oh, you're the guy who took my seat the other day," she said.

Again the damned seat.

"Yeah. Well, there was somebody I wanted to sit beside, that's all."

"No problem," she said. "I guess I shouldn't have made a big deal about it. I'm just used to sitting in the same seat. You know how you just get used to a certain things…"

"Yeah," I said, giving her a little smile.

"Exactly. But if there is somebody you want to sit beside, I can move and you can sit there."

"Thanks, I appreciate it. But it's your seat. I don't want to deprive you of your home," I said.

"Really, it's no problem. I'll just move back one and deprive somebody else of their home," she said with a smile.

"Sounds good."

Was I getting along with her? We were socializing, chit-chatting, flirting? No, I won't go that far. What was I doing? She seemed nice and cute, and she had a good sense of humour too. Maybe it wasn't really happening. Maybe I was still asleep.

"Have you been sleeping?" she asked.

"Why do you ask?"

"Your eyes tell me that you have just enjoyed a deep slumber," she said.

"Oh, yeah. I dozed off for some time."

"This book has put me to sleep a few times, too," she said.

"Do you think you know this stuff well?" I asked.

"Yeah, I think so. I need to study a lot more though. How about you?"

"I haven't studied anything. I'm going to fail in this test," I said.

"You won't fail."

I hate when people say that. I could fail. In fact, I thought failing was a big possibility.

"Maybe I could help you. What are you having problems with?" she asked.

"Pretty much everything," I said.

"Well, that narrows it down. At least we don't have to worry about covering the same topics."

"What do you mean, 'we'?" I asked.

"I mean I'll help you. Let's start on chapter four. It looks like you started reading that."

"Yeah, okay," I said.

And so it went. The *seat chor* started helping me with the OHT subject. And she kept helping and helping all afternoon. The subject wasn't nearly as boring when she was teaching it. Things made sense, they had purpose, and they took on new meaning. The whole time she taught me, I kept thinking of how little attention I must have paid in class in order to have missed all that information. And she kept getting more and more attractive all the time. The more I saw her, the more she looked attractive. I was glued to her and wanted to keep looking at her. The law of diminishing marginal utility was flawed for sure.

I watched the way her lips moved as she talked. But not just that; I soaked all she said in. It became easy to remember. I had never paid such close attention to someone discharging off such useless information in my entire life. I couldn't get enough of it. I wondered how I would have done in my school if she had been my teacher.

Every facial expression she made drew me in deeper; the way she squeezed her eyebrows together when she was thinking; the way her eyes opened wide when she smiled at me; the way she brushed her hair from her face and looped it behind her ear when she studied the book. I was hooked and I knew it. But I just told you about my rule no 7. I didn't reveal that I was interested.

Girls love a challenge, no matter what they tell you. Take it from me. I know what I'm talking about. So I acted completely casual the whole time. I looked interested in what she was saying, but I never overdid it.

"So how do you feel about this stuff now?" she asked.

"Good. I don't think I'll fail anymore," I said.

"You still have to study more, but I think we've made some progress," she said. "Yeah, well maybe we can get together again after I read this?

"Maybe tomorrow night?" I took my chance.

"Yeah, maybe. Let me give you my phone number and you can call me," she said.

"Sounds good."

"You know, this is totally embarrassing after we've been studying for the past few hours, but what's your name?" she asked.

I didn't want to tell her my name and I didn't want her to tell me hers. It seemed like we had the perfect chemistry going and I didn't want to spoil it. I think every guy dreams about having a great relationship with a girl without exchanging names and only using the phone in order to plan the next sexual engagement. But I guess that's just a dream.

"Ronnie Kapoor," I said.

"I'm Meghna Mathur."

"Pleasure to meet you," I said.

"Good to meet you, too."

We shook hands and smiled. I don't like these kinds of formal introductions, but they seem to be the socially acceptable thing to do. All that, 'Pleased to meet you,' crap. I wonder if anyone really means it. In my view, this is what really happens once a girl meets a guy.

Female Brain:

10% – I hope I was looking good.

30% – I hope he liked me.

25% – I hope we will meet again.

20% – I think he is a good guy.

14% – I think I can think about getting committed to him.

1% – I may have to sleep with him.

Male Brain:

97% – I want to sleep with her.

1% – When will I sleep with her?

1% – Where will I sleep with her?

1% – How do I sleep with her?

She asked me my number and WhatsApped me her number.

It was like getting the secret spell in harry potter to open the doors. I wanted to wave my wand and say "Alohomora" and the doors of her room would open to me.

The next day, I called Aaliya. But she didn't take my call. What was I supposed to do? I had my whole day planned around studying with her and now everything was screwed up. I needed to get the situation clear in my head before I could plot my next course of action. So I made a list of what all was to be done:

1) Aaliya's phone was on silent and she did not hear my call
2) There is an exam tomorrow
3) I have to fix Bhaskar's date
4) I need to meet Meghna
5) I have to prove that law of diminishing marginal utility is incorrect

There was only one thing to do in that situation: EAT.
In my view, life seems better if you have a full stomach.
I entered the kitchen to find DJ already eating. He was eating in typical DJ style – directly from the pan where the Maggi was about to get cooked. He always believed in simplicity, no silverware, no fancy crockery – directly from the pan.

"Hey DJ! What's up?" I asked.

"Nothing," he mumbled through a full mouth.

I went to the fridge and got out my favourite chicken tikka sandwich.

This kind of breakfast is a little expensive for a college student, but I couldn't live without it and my parents were paying the bill anyway.

I heated the sandwich in the microwave and just as I took a bite, I heard a knock on the door.

I walked to the door and opened it to see Prerna glaring at me. *Ab kya ho gaya isey?*

"I'm having a shitty day," she said as she walked past me.

"Why, what's up?"

"I got in a fight with my roommate this morning. I will tell you what happened later. But for now… just stay quiet and listen."

This was a girl fight that I wouldn't be able to relate to, I knew it. I don't know why girls bother to tell guys about stuff like that.

As I was busy munching my sandwich and Prerna was blabbering some crap right next to me, I heard another knock on the door. I wished it was Aaliya. After all, I had to study for the exam.

Bhaskar stood there bright-eyed and smiley faced when I opened the door.

"Hey man," he said, bouncing in. "What's going on?"

"Not much."

"Is she here?"

"No. I called her and she didn't pick up," I said.

"What?" The smile vanished immediately. "I thought you guys were going to study here today?"

"Well, what can I do? If she didn't pick up, she didn't pick up."

"This sucks," he said.

"Still going after that girl?" Prerna chimed in. "Why don't you give it up?"

"*Apney kaam sey kaam rakh*," said Bhaskar.

There were more random bullets flying in my apartment than in the movie *Shootout at Lokhandwala*.

I walked back and took another bite of my sandwich. Prerna and Bhaskar stared at me, perhaps waiting for me to say something.

"*Kya hai*?" I said, my mouth full of food. By the way, that is usually the appropriate response when anyone is staring at you. They both looked away instantly.

DJ walked in and sat down in front of the couch, switching the television on.

"Don't you ever do anything?" Prerna woofed at him.

"Shut up," he said in a monotone voice. I loved it when he talked like that.

"Don't tell me to shut up. I'm leaving. I can't stand this guy." Prerna said and quickly walked out of the apartment, banging the door behind her.

That's why I liked DJ so much. Because when it came to rescuing me, he unknowingly always helped me.

The phone rang just then and jolted me out of my thoughts.

"Hello?" I asked.

"Hi, is Ronnie there?"

"This is Ronnie," I said.

"Hi, this is Aaliya. I was taking a shower when you called. Just saw your message. Do you want to get together and study?"

What perfect timing! I imagined Aaliya standing in her towel with glistening skin and water dripping from her hair. Yes I wanted to get together and study her. Deeply.

"Yeah, sure," I said.

"How about I meet you on the first floor in the library."

"Sounds good. When?" I asked.

"I'll be ready in the next fifteen minutes or so. Then I'm going to head over to the library and I'll see you when you get there," she said.

"I'm ready now. In fact, this would be a good time for me to get out of my place. I'll see you in about thirty minutes then."

It was almost too easy. I hate when they practically throw themselves at you like that. I wasn't even sure if she was actually in the bathroom when I called her. Maybe she wanted to specifically tell me that she was attending my call in just a towel.

"Was that Aaliya?" Bhaskar asked.

"Yeah."

"Are you guys going to study?"

"Yeah," I said.

"Here?"

"No. At the library."

"Even better. I can come to the library with you. This will be awesome," he said.

I wasn't so sure that it would be awesome. It could be fascinating. Possibly entertaining. But not awesome.

Bhaskar chewed my ears the whole way to the library. He was like a wimpy Japanese school girl that had just been awarded the prize for the most beautiful eyes. Anyway, he was jabbering on about little things I could ask him about so he could tell some interesting story, but I didn't listen to most of what he was saying. For whatever reason – and I really don't know why – I was thinking about the *seat chor*.

I tried to fight it out, ignoring her images forming in my mind – her smile, and eyes, and the way she talked. But the more I tried to ignore, the more her thoughts invaded my senses.

That wasn't good. I was on a mission. I couldn't get distracted.

I was there again, at the steps of the library. Bhaskar and I made it up to the first floor and sure enough, there was Aaliya, head in the books and looking fabulous.

"Hi, Aaliya," I said as I approached the table.

"Hi," she said, smiling.

"Hi, Aaliya," Bhaskar said.

I instantly felt stupid. Although she returned his hello, her face told the real story. It said, "*Yeh dhakkan tumharey sath kyun aaya hai*? I thought it was just going to be the two of us? Isn't he the same guy who is always waiting for you when we come out of class? Are you guys dating or something?"

So there I was with a beautiful girl wearing a confused look on her face and my desperate, pathetic friend, waiting for me to do something. I wanted to remind Bhaskar about rule number five: Never use a friend to hook up with the person you like. Your friend might just betray you.

Since Bhaskar didn't know this rule yet, and I hadn't enlightened him, I decided to give him the benefit of doubt. Another chance.

"Aaliya, you remember Bhaskar, don't you?" I asked.

"Yeah, sure." She replied coldly.

"Are you ready to study?"

"Yeah, have you studied?" she asked.

"A little bit."

Of course I was lying. I felt like a professor after the study session with Meghna, but I didn't want Aaliya to feel left out.

"I didn't really study," she said. "I gave a quick read to most of it but I have to finish reading the last chapter before I go back and really start cramming it."

"No problem. When you're ready, we can quiz each other about it. I'll go over my notes," I said.

"Okay, awesome."

She said it was awesome. Maybe Bhaskar was right about it being awesome. I looked over at him and he gave me a look of approval. I guess he liked the way things were going. I guess he wasn't aware that there wasn't anything going on between him and Aaliya.

I opened my notebook, which was kind of funny in itself, because I hardly took any notes in class. I flipped through page after page of bad notes, sketches, some scribbled phone numbers, some saliva-stained pages, and so on. I didn't want to open the many pages of copied notes that Meghna had run off for me on the Xerox and have to explain them to Aaliya.

As I put my notebook to one side and reached for my textbook, I noticed Bhaskar looking at Aaliya. Oh, he was breaking rule number 7. He should have just ignored her and followed the rule. But then again, he didn't know the rule existed.

Just when I opened my book, I found my eyes wandering towards her as well. I looked at her thin manicured fingers as they skimmed through the pages; her strawberry lips sucking in the pencil. I wondered if the pencil was too thin for her.

I started having bad thoughts and that's always a good start, for something else, not studies. I knew I shouldn't have been thinking like that about her, but the thoughts came anyway. I started to form a plan to get Aaliya while keeping it a secret from Bhaskar. I suddenly felt that stabbing my friend in the back was the thing to do. I didn't feel good about it. I wasn't happy. I'm not made of stone, for God's sake. But she was just so beautiful that I felt myself turning to the dark side.

I opened my book and started going over everything that Meghna and I had studied the day before. Or rather all that Meghna had taught me the day before. The entire syllabus came back to me. And so did the way she talked, the way she smelled, the way she smiled.

"Okay, I think I'm ready," Aaliya said. "Let's quiz each other."

"All right. Let's start on chapter four."

Aaliya and I started talking about the same things that Meghna and I had gone over the previous day. I was surprised at how much she knew, despite her claims that she hadn't studied enough and knew little. As we went along, though I was the one coaching her, guiding her, shaping her young mind, she still managed to teach me a thing or two. She was impressed with how much I knew. I could see that on her face. She looked at me in awe, as if she was discovering a whole new me that she wanted to get to know better. Bhaskar could sense it, too. He tried to jump in once in a while with some clever witticism, but usually just fell flat on his face.

Aaliya and I were so deep into our studying and quizzing, along with subtle flirting, that we didn't realise when Bhaskar had left. *Arey yeh kab chala gaya?*

"Where's Bhaskar?" I asked.

"He left a while ago. Don't you remember? He said goodbye."

"I must have been looking in my book," I said.

That wasn't good. I had to fix this mess and do what I set out to do in the first place.

"Bhaskar's a really great guy. What do you think of him?" I asked.

"He seems nice."

Oh, nice. That's never what you want to hear. Guys and girls all want to be cool or sexy or tough or unruly or hot or whatever…but never nice.

"I think he likes you. He wants to ask you out," I said. *Mainey apna farz poora kar diya.*

"Oh, yeah," she said disinterestedly, never looking up from her book.

"How about I give him your phone number and he can call you?" *Ek aur baar try kiya maine Bhaskar ke liye.*

"I think we should get back to studying," she said.

"It's just a phone number," I said in a bouncy voice, trying to ease the situation.

"I don't even know him," she said.

"Point taken. Okay. Where were we? Chapter five?"

You can't say I didn't try. I did my best. What more could Bhaskar want from me?

Aaliya and I continued to study, but it wasn't the same. In fact, there wasn't much of anything. We wrapped it up, said our goodbyes, and I headed back to my apartment.

I cruised into the apartment to find DJ sitting on the couch, watching TV. As always.

"Dude, the guys are coming down. Party this weekend?" he said, not turning to look at me.

"Cool," I said.

DJ's cryptic statement meant that his friends from Chandigarh were going to be staying at our place Friday night. Therefore, we would be having another party at our apartment. This was good. Parties at our apartment were always fun. There were plenty of chicks and the alcohol never ran dry. We didn't even have to worry about cleaning up after the party. We never cleaned anyway.

And then an idea hit me like a bolt of lightning. Party at our place. Bhaskar and Aaliya together in the right atmosphere. It could all come together. Bhaskar wouldn't hate me because he would see that I was still working for him. Aaliya is a babe, and since girls always travel in packs, she would bring some of her babe friends with her. The plan seemed perfect!

I burst awake to find that my iPhone was vibrating and rotating on the table and the alarm ringtone was blaring. I had completely forgotten about the test I was about to take. I took my shower, got something to eat, and brushed my teeth, all while thinking about the bullshit I was to be tested on. I stuffed my backpack with all the required material and ran into the hall in the last few precious seconds before the test started.

Professor Sharma was closing the door as I ran up.

"One last passenger before we take off. Come in, come in," he said cheerfully as I made my way past him, huffing and puffing.

"Just in time," I said.

I quickly scanned the room and sure enough, Meghna had left a seat for me. The day was already looking up. It was the right day to take a test.

I said hello to Aaliya and Meghna, in that order, and they returned the greeting pleasantly enough.

Sometimes I even impressed myself. *By God ki kasam, kya faadu banda hoon main yaar!*

"Did you do any more studying?" Meghna asked me.

79

I turned away from Aaliya so as to not attract attention to the fact that I had another babe on the hook.

"Yeah, a little," I said.

Our conversation was nipped in the bud. Prof. Sharma looked quite proud of himself as he stood in front of the class.

"Shall we go on with the test?" he asked.

I wanted to say, "No let's go and drink beer." I never understood why teachers asked such stupid questions and why my parents paid for this shit.

He finally started handing out the dreaded white sheets with horizontal blue lines in which we were supposed to write our tests.

"Now, you don't have to answer all of them. Read the instructions. Only three of the five," he said.

Usually I was the first one to finish an exam. But today was different. I was confident that I would be writing up to the last minute. My determination knew no bounds. My head was full of knowledge and I was ready to fill pages with it.

I was like Milkha Singh waiting for the race to start, like Salman waiting to dance, like Malika Sherawat waiting to undress....I guess you got the idea.

I looked around. I could see two distinct groups. Girls were acting in a different way and guys totally different. I could actually write a thesis on "Girl's and Guy's insights in an examination hall." It would go like this:

Things most girls do in an exam hall:
Tuck hair behind ears
Answer questions....

Change the empty refill
Think and write ... then ...
Ask teacher for an extra sheet
Again keep writing & answering questions ...

Things most boys do in an exam hall:
First look at how many girls are there in the same hall
Check out if the professor is female…then check her out
Look at the exam paper .... ???!!!!!…
Count how many doors & windows are there in the hall
Revise the location of chits in the pockets
Little writing then…
See the brand name of the pen
Ask the teacher to explain questions
Look at the watch…
Regret wasting the last night studying
Finally thinking to study well in the next exam

And After the exam….

The girls would look like they've had a hard time with the exam. They'd say, "You know, the exam was a bit hard. I don't know what I did, I am afraid to fail." (That means 75+ marks.)

The boys look like they have everything under control. They'd say, "It was not too bad, you know." (Which means they may just get passing marks!)

The professor handed me the question paper and I came back to my senses. The first question seemed difficult and confusing, so I moved on to the second question.

Unfortunately, the second question was also hard and confusing, but not as bad as the first, so I read it again. On the second time around, it did in fact seem as difficult and confusing as the first one.

I glanced around quickly and noticed that everyone else had already started writing. Sweat started to gather on my brow. Breathing became a struggle. My shirt felt constricting around my neck.

Milkha Singh disappeared, Salman went for a nap, Malika Sherawat wore her clothes back.

I had to pull myself together. After all, I only had to answer three of them. There was a chance that the next three would be the ones for me, so I pressed on. The third one: difficult and confusing. The fourth: worse. The fifth: hope! Yes, the fifth question. Maybe it was a good idea to start bottom to top in the question paper and not top to bottom as per my rule number two for girls.

I took a dive into writing, remembering what Meghna's lips had said.

Then something broke my concentration. Aaliya crossed her legs. Twice.

Question five. I had to get back to work. My pen started to move across the paper frantically. But I checked its brand. Parker. Shit. I had to concentrate. I started writing again. Everything Meghna and I had talked about came flooding out of my brain. The ideas started to flow. I wrote and wrote and wrote some more. I was poetry in motion. After about fifteen minutes of that, I decided I was finished with question five.

Aaliya uncrossed and re-crossed her legs again. *Yaar yeh aisey kyu kar rahi hai. Isko meri koi chinta nahin hai.* I rubbed my forehead and told myself not to look. I looked anyway. Again.

There were two more questions to go. Question four was the least threatening of those that remained. I knew if I could just come up with a strong starting statement and an ending statement, everything else would fall into place. And that's what I did. Since I hadn't been the best student over the years, I had to rely on other skills. I remembered Air Supply's song *'Making love out of nothing at all'*. That was what I was going to do.

I finished the question and looked at my watch. My watch told me that there were only fifteen minutes left. I fought to concentrate on the test. I now knew none of the answers, so I just chose number three and started writing. My pen started moving over the paper without my having any control over it. I watched myself write, not knowing what word was going to appear on the next line, or next page. I just wrote everything else that Meghna had taught me in the final answer, hoping something would fit in. Before I knew it, Professor Sharma spoke up.

"Okay, that's it! Pass your papers to the front."

I, along with everyone still left in the room, scrambled to write one last concluding sentence. This last concluding sentence is usually the most important.

It's like the last *papdi* you have, after having ten *golgappas*. It's like the last push before an orgasm. It's like setting your hair the last time before you leave for a party. You know what I mean.

I scribbled the concluding line as the professor came in and literally snatched the paper from me. I turned around and Meghna smiled at me.

"How did you do?" she asked.

"Okay. How about you?" (Which meant, I may just get passing marks!)

"I don't know. It was harder than I thought it would be," she said. (Which meant 75+ marks!)

I got up and started to walk out with her.

"I'm so glad it's over," she said. "Thankfully my parents are not in town tonight. So I plan to go out tonight and blow off some steam."

"Sounds like what I need, too." After all, I had studied the last two days in a row. That's more than I had done in…I don't remember how many years.

"Where are you planning to go?" she asked.

It was a difficult question. I gave it a deep thought and decided to give the most apt answer.

"Maybe Matchbox lounge in Hauz Khas village," I said.

"That's great. How about we meet there at 8 p.m.?" she said.

"Sure, I'll see you there."

Aaliya watched as Meghna and I walked out together. She was jealous. I could smell it. Smelling jealousy was another one of my talents.

> **Rule 8: Get overfriendly with other girls in front of the girl you want. This will make her jealous and she would want you even more.**

Aaliya was a few steps ahead of us and I tried to keep pace with her while talking to Meghna. A guy always has to keep his options open.

I kept looking at the clock and waited for it to strike 8. As the clock struck 7.45, I left my apartment dressed in a simple white t-shirt and denims. It was my favourite pair of jeans, because it was the easiest to take off. And tonight, I guessed, it had to be taken off.

I reached Matchbox and squeezed past a couple walking out. I bumped into some guy in a T-shirt that read *"Don't want me yet? Have another Drink."* He had something there.

I looked around scanning for Meghna, but I didn't make it that obvious. It was a retro, rockabilly inside. Glass walls, a gigantic bar, red-vinyl booths, and a high decibel JBL music system pumping out awesome music. I dug this place. But Meghna was nowhere to be seen.

While I was busy chatting with a few people and trying to show that I was having a great time, a shadow fell over the table. I looked up and my gaze froze on Meghna's beautiful face. She had actually taken the pain to dress up, and looked stunning. She could have made any guy go gaga.

I had realized in the library session that she was beautiful. But not like this. Not with sleek, perfect hair styled immaculately, drawn on her face into a sculpted bun at the nape of her neck, her make-up so subtle that it was as if she were wearing none, the shimmer of pearls at her earlobes, her white top and pink coloured skirt making her look dazzling.

"Hey, you are looking gorgeous!" I said, shaking her hand.

She just smiled back as I held her hand for longer than normal. For pretty long actually.

"Want some beer?

She nodded.

"I'll get some."

So I left Meghna and went to grab two beers from the bar. It was crowded with folks smoking cigarettes and grabbing their drinks and swearing at the bartender to quickly hand their drinks. I burrowed my way toward the bar, which was sealed away for me by a lair of people. Miraculously, the silver lining appeared as a guy came out with his drinks, and pushed myself into the space created by him. I smiled at the beauty of it and began the game wherein I tried to catch the bartender's attention. Thanks to my first rule of keeping the right contacts in the right place, the bartender took notice of me and quickly handed my drinks over to me.

In almost an hour, both of us had swallowed a lot of booze. I stood with Meghna in one corner with our bellies full of beer. She was all taut and pretty and wasted, her lipstick smeared in the sexiest of ways.

It was time to go. I walked out of the lounge along with her.

"Where do you live?" I asked.

"I live in Safdarjang Enclave." She laughed and pushed her hair out of her face

I looked for a cab but there was no cab around. I clicked Hola cabs app icon on my iPhone and there it was. The map showed that a cab was just five minutes and fifty metres away. I simply clicked and booked it.

I wish I could get a girlfriend so easily too.

Imagine there was an app called "I am horny" which would show all the people nearby who were horny at that point of time. I could simply click and check out the profile and go and make out with her. Well I am not sure if such an app would be possible in India, but then I still believe it's a great idea.

I scratched at an itch on my neck. The cab arrived and we pushed ourselves inside it. Meghna kept giving some directions to the cab driver, which I am sure were wrong because we reached Safdarjang forty minutes later. The place won't be half the distance away. I looked at the bill and then paid off the driver with a heavy heart. This dating game sure involved some investment, but then it also had its own returns.

As we stepped down from the cab, she left my hand and started running. She was pointing in some direction and I hurried behind her.

It wasn't far, which was good for me since I'm totally out of shape. I don't look like I'm out of shape, mind you, but you won't see me running any marathons in the near future.

We reached a cream coloured building which had two flats on each floor and a total of three such floors. There were many such identical buildings placed next to each other like a set of books placed neatly in a shelf.

We climbed up the stairs to the first floor. We jumped the last two feet into her house and laughed at ourselves.

"Come on," she said, as she opened the door.

We entered a dark flat and I followed Meghna to her room. She opened her room and switched on the lights.

"Here we are," she said.

The first thing I noticed was its remarkable cleanliness. Everything was neat and orderly to the point of being immaculate.

The beds were made, the desk was clean, and the floor sparkling. When I compared my apartment to this place of beauty, I realized that guys and girls live in different worlds. I think if it weren't for the sexual attraction between us, we would never talk to each other.

I found Meghna standing in front of me, grabbing the bottom of my t-shirt.

"Here, take that off," she said. She pulled it up and over my head before I had a chance to react.

Her eyes looked straight into mine, only a few inches from my face now. Before I knew it, I had bridged the small gap between us and found myself in a lip lock with her. She kissed me back. We skipped straight from the gentle, "I want to show you how much I care about you" kisses, to the "I want to rip your clothes off" kisses. She threw her arms around my shoulders. My right hand found its way to her hip and my left stayed on the bed for support.

It wasn't long before my mouth left hers and I made my way down her neck. The neck was always a fun place to kiss… only because of what it led to. I slid down to the upper chest, but didn't waste much time there. It was more of an interlude than anything. And then I arrived at the landscape and started kissing. It was heaven.

Meghna kicked her shoes off and I did the same. I moved her up on the bed. Once we were fully on the bed and comfortable, her hands went down and started to undo my pants. I, in turn, went after her skirt and we pulled each other's lowers off quickly. There nothing remaining between us now.

The sexual encounter was great and just like the last sentence in the exam, I gave the last push and said, "Aaliya, you are awesome."

That did it. Meghna threw me off the bed and started throwing things at me. It took me a minute to realize what was happening. Oh Shit! I had verbalized my fantasy and called her Aaliya. Before I could try and take a grip of the situation, I found myself standing out of her door.

Because OHT class was on my mind all morning, I left my apartment on time and arrived at class a few minutes before it started. I was quite muddled in my head because of last night. As I walked towards the class, my stomach turned in knots. I was, in fact, afraid to see Meghna and Aaliya. I should have stayed at my apartment. There were more than just butterflies in my stomach. There was a whole bunch of animals creating a stampede. My feet took me to the class without my control and, before I knew it, I was in the classroom.

Aaliya was in the middle of writing something and didn't notice that I had come in. Meghna, on the other hand, did something particularly terrible. She looked up, noticed me, and quickly turned her head to look out the window.

The seat in front of Meghna was vacant. I looked to the back of the room and noticed that my old seat was vacant as well. I decided that my old seat would be the safer bet for today. I walked to the back and slid into my familiar chair. Aaliya never saw me. Meghna didn't turn around to see where I went.

Professor Sharma entered the room and tossed his bag beside the desk. Some people slowly took out notebooks and pens, but most of the class didn't pay any attention to his entrance. I paid attention. I had little else to pay attention to. There were no short skirts or great legs in my immediate vicinity.

As dreadful a feeling as it was to start the class, which I knew I would spend looking at the backs of Meghna's and Aaliya's heads, there was one thing I could count on – I was not going to get my test results today. Never in the history of my stint in college had a teacher evaluated the tests in a day .

"I have your test results," Sharma said, hoisting a stack of papers in the air.

By God ki kasam, aaj toh lag gyi bencho.

"I guess that doesn't make everyone happy," Sharma said, looking at me, "but here they are."

I guess thinking about his classes was the only thing he had in his life. Giving us marks must have been a big orgasmic accomplishment for him. Didn't he have a life to live?

He started to call out names and one by one people walked to the front of the class to take their results. As I waited for my name to be called, I felt like a man getting down from a horse to get married. The end of life.

"Aaliya Oberoi," Sharma said. Aaliya walked up to the front to receive her test. As she turned around and looked at her marks, she made no evident facial expressions to signify whether it was good or bad. That usually meant bad. I waited some more.

Name after name was called out, but still not mine. *Pata nahi mera number kab ayega?*

Meghna's name was called and I watched as she took her results, but again, no clear facial expression. That wasn't a warm feeling. The two people I studied with weren't smiling. I watched them as they flipped through the pages with emotionless faces.

"Ronnie Kapoor," Sharma said.

"Yes," I said walking to the front. I went up to him, grabbed my test, and got back to my seat as quickly as I could.

I didn't open it. The full range of emotions raced through me.

What if it was 70%? What if it was 30%? Things were already bad enough and I didn't think I could take it. I wasn't ready for this.

I slowly looked at my paper. On the top was written the following:

41/100. You stated a few facts and theories so it was clear that you must have studied some chapters. However, your answers did not flow in a well thought-out manner.

I passed. *Oye hoye, balle balley...chak dey fattey... bruuuah....* In only two days of studying I went from a sure 0 to a decent 41. Okay, so I wasn't going to win a scholarship. I could live with that.

Prof. Sharma finished handing out the papers and started giving a speech about the results. The same about how some people could have done better and 'I expect this' and 'I expect that'. The same speech that I've heard a hundred times. The salary of teachers should be deducted every time they repeated their speech. They just make money for the things they say over and over again.

"Well, can we now get started with the next chapter?" Sharma said.

"No, we should rather get started with some hash to celebrate this event," I wanted to say, but obviously did not. There was enough shit to swim out of already.

Another forty minutes of dragging lecture later, the class ended. I decided to follow Meghna out of the room.

I caught up with her at the door.

"Hi. How did you do on the test?" I asked.

She half-turned. "Oh, I did okay."

I think she was still annoyed from last night. She was pretending like she didn't care about me or the test, so that she could end the conversation and get away from me. I knew that trick. But we were in the corridor, and since that was public domain, she couldn't escape.

"I passed. I'm not too happy about the score, but it's okay I guess," I said.

"I got 75," she said.

Mere ko pata tha iskey 75 ayengey. "Hey, that's great. You really seemed like you knew your stuff when we studied together," I said, trying to bring up some positive memory.

"Yeah, I'm happy with it," she said.

We reached the front door of the building and walked out into the excitement of campus life.

"So," I said. "What would you think about going out tonight?"

"Sorry, I can't. I'm busy tonight," she said.

Ouch. That meant, '*Main bilkul free hoon par tumharey sath kaheen nahi jaungi.*'

"Maybe some other time?" I asked.

I couldn't believe those words came out of my mouth. She had just slammed the door on me and now I was knocking again. I had always made fun of other guys for doing the same thing. Now I found myself acting like the idiot I swore I'd never become. I already knew what she would say before she said it.

"Yeah, maybe," she said.

Of course that's what she said. It's the same response that Sita would have given to Ravan. When Ravan would have asked her out, she would have said no. Then on his insistence, she would have said, yeah maybe.

It was all just a polite way of saying, 'There's no way in hell I'm ever going out with you because you're a pathetic loser.'

Well Ravan had the guts to just pick Sita up and take her in his ancient helicopter. I wish I could do the same.

"Okay, bye," she said. Her way of saying, '*Chal nikal chutiye.*'

It was a lazy Friday morning and I lay with the pillow over my head, trying to block the sun out. I had just awoken from my recurring fantasy dream, wherein I made love to two hot babes on a beach-side.

My throat was parched and I looked around for a bottle of water. I grabbed the bottle and put my lips to it; the sun shone right in my eyes. It was a nice sunny day. I remembered Honey Singh's song '*Aaj blue hai paani paani, aur din bhi sunny sunny saani...*' I wondered how he would have cleared his English exams where *paani* and *sunny/saani* have the same spelling and pronunciation.

You know, I would like life much more if we could do away with Mondays, Tuesdays, Wednesdays and Thursdays. Not much good happened in those four days. Except Matchbox happy hours, of course.

As I went through my morning routine, I noticed that DJ wasn't around. There was no way he would have gotten up early to go somewhere. He had probably never come home last night; would have slept at some girl's place. That was annoying. Sex was one of those things that if *you* aren't getting, you don't want anyone else to get it either. It is like a person's salary: you always feel that the other guy is getting more than you.

I walked out the door and off to class. I felt pretty good and had resolved to talk to Aaliya. I'm not sure why I decided that. Maybe because when I looked into the mirror that morning, I liked what I saw. Or maybe because I could use the party as an excuse to talk to her. Plus, Sri Sri Honey Singh had made me believe it was a *saani* day. Or maybe because any excuse was a good excuse to talk to a girl who had legs like hers. Whatever the case, I walked into the class a good five minutes before it started. But that's when I made a shocking discovery: the only seat that was open around Aaliya was the one right behind her. There was someone sitting in front of Meghna. Therefore, I had to sit right across Meghna, which was behind Aaliya, which is exactly what I wanted to avoid. *By God ki kasam, lag gayi bhai aaj toh.*

If I could sit in front of Meghna, then we could ignore each other peacefully and I could talk to Aaliya.

I felt a lump in my throat as I moved towards the seat. I tossed my backpack beside the desk and tried to pretend that I hadn't seen Meghna. She, in turn, pretended that she hadn't seen me. I wondered if she was actually pretending, or she hadn't noticed me at all. And if she hadn't noticed me, then I wanted her to notice me. At least then I could get the satisfaction of ignoring her. What was I thinking?

"Hi," Aaliya said, turning around.

She caught me totally off guard since I was very busy ignoring Meghna. After all, it was a very difficult task. "Hi," I said.

That's when Professor Sharma walked into the room with his hair a mess, struggling to carry a stack of miscellaneous papers under his arm. He was quite the spectacle.

"Here we go," Aaliya whispered, turning to face the professor.

This allowed me to get back to ignoring Meghna. Not an easy task, mind you. I had a burning desire to look over at her, just a glance to see what she was up to. Plus, I wanted to see if she would look back at me.

Why did I have a burning desire to do this? I have no idea. *Sach mein.*

When any relationship comes to an end, the person who makes the last contact is in the weaker position. It could be an sms, a WhatsApp/ Facebook post, a phone call, a statement, or a glance. But as it stood, I had made the last contact, thereby putting me in the weaker position. She held the dominant position in the post-relationship relationship. I wanted the better position. If I looked at her, and she looked back at me, and I looked away before she had a chance to look away, then I would be in the dominant position. It seems immature, but it is extremely important in the world of dating.

"We are going to start a new chapter today," Professor Sharma said.

I couldn't have cared less about the new chapter. Instead, I started to execute a plan to get the last contact in the post-relationship relationship. I looked in front to see Aaliya's long, dark hair flowing down her shoulders. I admired it for just a second but then, without notice, jerked my head to the left to look at Meghna. She had been looking into her notebook, but in response to my sudden movement, she looked over at me, smiled a half-smile, and turned back to her notebook – all before I had a chance to look away. Damn! She had thrown me off with an unexpected smile. She still had the dominant position and more. Not only was I still the one to make last contact, but her smile proved that she was more dominant and more mature.

Class continued on with Sharma chanting some mantras from the new chapter of god knows what, and Aaliya crossed-uncrossed her legs thrice.

When the class finally ended, everyone put their registers away at lightning speed to head for the door.

"I thought that would never end," I said to Aaliya.

"I know what you mean," she said.

I followed her out the door. We made it out to the crowded corridor where I forced my way into the crowd to walk beside her.

"I wanted to invite you for a party tonight at my place. 70 B, Shanti Niketan. My friend and I throw some cool parties."

"Well, let me think," she said.

"Oh come on, little partying on Friday night will do you good." I smiled at her.

"Ok. I'll be there. Wait a minute. 70 B, Shanti Niketan? Is this the same party organized by some guy called DJ?"

"Yeah, but how do you know that? He is my friend and stays with me at the same address."

"He has invited some of my friends too. I guess it will be fun. I'll see you there," she said. "My friends are looking forward to it. Is Prerna going to be there?"

"Yeah. And so is Bhaskar," I added.

"Oh, your corridor friend! Anyway, at least I'll know a few people in the party then," she said.

Aaliya was the kind of girl who knew a lot of people wherever she went.

"I need to get to my next class," said Aaliya. "I guess I'll see you at the party."

"Okay, bye," I said and watched her disappear into the crowd.

The day and the week finally came to a close, and I headed home. I walked into my apartment but I kind of wished I was back at the college because then at least I'd have something to do.

So, having nothing to do, I found myself in my room, looking at my iPhone for no particular reason. I saw Ruchika's number, Meghna's number, and Aaliya's number and many other names which I had not called for a while now. I thought about the things I loved about girls and why I needed to fuck around with more and more girls. It was like an addictive game of Candy Crush. You just can't stop playing it. It's like a competition with yourself.

I opened the Facebook profiles of each of the girls I had slept with and kept fantasizing about a few I couldn't sleep with. There was Aaliya's photograph in a bikini. Wow she looked so hot! With this great feeling in my head and my hand under the bedsheets, I don't remember when I finished and when I dozed off.

❖

Everyone was supposed to come by 8. Since DJ's friends had come from Chandigarh earlier than that, I was already feeling tipsy by the time people started coming. After a few shots and some mugs of beer, all my worries, fantasies, phone numbers, test results vanished from my memory. There were plenty of beautiful girls and enough alcohol to go around.

Prerna had come to the party, but I hadn't had the time to talk to her since her arrival. Bhaskar looked nervous from the minute he showed up. He knew Aaliya would soon be walking in with her friends and he would be on her like a dog on a juicy bone. *Bow Bow.*

I had just finished doing a round of tequila shots with DJ and the guys when I heard a voice behind me.

"Hi," the female voice said.

It was a voice I immediately recognized but couldn't place.

I turned around to see Ruchika. Don't ask me what her last name was. I can never remember.

"Hi, how are you?" I asked.

I have to admit I felt pretty stupid. I had just seen her phone number in the afternoon in my iPhone. I had even spent time on her Facebook page. I should have called her.

"Hey, Ruchika," DJ said from the other side of the table.

He walked over to her and they hugged. I was surprised to know that even DJ knew her.

As I watched her hugging him, I had the definite feeling that I wouldn't be waking up next to her the following morning. I needed to drink more, I guess.

By nine o'clock, most of the people that were going to come to the party were there; everyone except Aaliya, that is. I remembered talking to several girls. There was a lot of laughing…on my part, at least. There was a lot of showing off on the part of all the guys. As usual, the showing off usually came in the form of making fun of each other and trying to make the girls laugh. *In short, ek dusrey ki leney mein lagey huey they ladke style marne ke liye.*

This brings us to the next rule:

> **Rule 9: Be the first one to make fun of other guys in front of the girls.**

First, a guy makes fun of the other guys around him to make them look stupid and make himself look superior. This makes them appear less smart to the girls. Second, he finds out which girls laugh at his jokes and frowns at other guy's jokes. This gives an indication as to which girl he could try his luck with. If a girl is interested, she will laugh at whatever he says. The process of guys making fun of each other is an essential ritual in the holy process. When I say holy process, I am referring to the process one must go through in order to make a girl interested in sex for that night.

Anyway, while I was deep into the holy process with one of the girls standing near me, in walked Meghna. I tried to remember if I had invited her. My brain was working in slow motion and it took me a minute to get my nuts and bolts tightened. Then DJ greeted her near the door. The guy knew everybody. It was all I needed. I quickly lost interest in the girl I was talking to, which didn't really matter because I didn't even know her name. Like a fool, I approached Meghna.

"Hey, what's up?" I said.

"Hi," said Meghna

"I didn't think I'd see you here," I said.

"I didn't know you would be here either."

"I live here," I said.

"Oh, okay," she said. "Well, maybe I'll talk to you later."

"Yeah, cool," I said. I actually thought she meant that she would talk to me later. It shows the extent of my confused state. I was behaving like Bhaskar. I was feeling a bit dehydrated. I went to the refrigerator and pulled out the only water bottle on the top shelf. It was empty. Crap. I kept it back and plucked out a pint of beer from the over-stacked lot inside.

Aaliya walked through the door at 10.30 p.m. In that moment it seemed everyone stopped talking to look at Aaliya and the four friends who she came with. All of them were incredibly hot, just slightly less hot than Aaliya, but still hotter than any of the hot girls already at the party. This also caused everyone to make comments, at least in their heads – which is where the best comments are made anyway – and only then continue on with their conversations, or drinking, or card games, or whatever they were doing. Some people stopped what they were doing in order to greet the pack of babes as they made their way in the room.

"Aaliya, what's up?"

"Oh, hi Ronnie!"

At a time like that, when four hot girls you've never met before are looking at you while you talk to the hot leader of the group, it is best to keep talking to that leader, making you look incredibly good while waiting to be introduced at the proper time. The last thing you would ever say in a situation like that is, 'Hey, who are these people with you. Why don't you introduce me to your friends?'

"Hey, who are these people with you? Why don't you introduce me to your friends?" I asked. *Oops! Did I just say that?*

Aaliya politely turned to her friends and introduced them. I couldn't remember even one name. So I named them in my head – pouty lips, big boobs, sexy slim and blue eyes. Now I would remember them. They seemed like Charlie's Angels; the only difference was that I was more interested in Charlie. I mean not Charlie, Aaliya. The booze played games with my mind and words, but I think you got the point.

And that's when all the alcohol in my head started to betray me.

"Where are you guys from?" I asked.

Sexy Slim made a sour face.

"We're from here and now we want to go there." She pointed towards DJ who was playing a game of drinking maximum tequila shots.

At that point I noticed that the other girls, including Aaliya, had moved on, away from me. And even though it was good to have Sexy Slim one-on-one, there were several things working against me at that point. First, she was hot, which always put any guy under pressure. Second, I was wasted, so my brain was having trouble forming thoughts and remembering my rules. Third, she seemed like she hadn't had a single drink, which probably made her think I was a complete idiot. Fourth, she was hot. I know I already said that, but like I told you, I was wasted. Her hotness was intimidating and distracting at the same time.

"Oh," I said. "Yeah." I was already running out of things to say and I had just started.

"Where's the booze?" she asked.

"It's in the refrigerator in the kitchen," I said.

Sexy Slim turned toward the kitchen. I was just about to ask her what course she was pursuing and which college was she in, when I stopped myself. I turned back into the living room, figuring I'd have better chances with the girls I knew or at least who were as drunk as I was.

Warna frequency match hona mushkil tha.

People moved past me in blurred masses. I saw everything in threes, or maybe fours. It had been several hours since my introduction to Aaliya's friends. My tongue had gone numb much earlier in the evening, after the first joint I had, but I suddenly took note of its numbness after the fourth or maybe the fifth joint. I had downed some water earlier I think, but my mouth was totally dry at that point. I vaguely remembered staggering and bumping into a few people somewhere in there, but I don't think they cared because they were as out of it as I was.

I tried looking at the clock, and guessed it to be 3 a.m.

That's when I saw Prerna across the room, sitting in a chair, talking to someone across from her. I went for help.

"I think I'm dying."

"You'll live."

"Seriously. *Main chala Prernaaaa.*"

Maybe she believed me the second time I said it, because she seemed to take pity on me. She got off her chair and looked me in the eyes. The few people who were still left were starting to lie around the apartment at that point, staking their claims for the night. I hoped Prerna would take care of me as she had done so many times in the past.

I sort of remember throwing my arm around her. And I sort of remember her walking with me for a little while. Then she helped me sit down.

I don't think I thanked her, but I could sense that she walked away. Before I knew it, my eyes were closing and I drifted off into that wonderful world of sleep.

I felt my cheek lying against something that felt like cold glass before I even opened my eyes. I held my head upright and wiped the drool from my mouth. The beer pitcher was beside me and I could feel its imprint on my face. I wasn't sure how long I had been there, probably about an hour or so.

I realized I still didn't have any girl for the night. I decided to look around for Aaliya as this was the night when we had to be together in bed. I had invested enough time on her.

Thanks to DJ, we did not have locks in any of the doors. One drunk night we had spent four hours breaking every lock of the house as we wanted an open door policy. Well, the policy wasn't working tonight; I was cursed every time I tried opening the door.

I stood up to walk to my bedroom and noted the remarkable number of people sleeping around the apartment. I stopped for a second to see if I recognized them. Most of them were DJ's friends, scattered around on the floor wherever they could find space. Just before my room, I entered the guest room and noticed a guy and a girl sleeping on the floor. Those people looked familiar. As I made my way over, I saw that it was DJ and Meghna. My mind was slow to react as I looked at them a little too long.

Was I happy? No. But I can't say I was disappointed either.

I had my chance and I blew it. There was one thing that I wondered about. Why would DJ sleep on the floor instead of his own bed? That was the real story. I walked over to the bedrooms and, instead of going to my own, I cracked open the door to DJ's room. There was Bhaskar, sound asleep with his arm draped around Aditi. He was snuggled up against her and the two of them looked quite content. *Chalo acha hua.*

Aaliya was never right for him; she was for guys like me. Bhaskar had the real thing with Aditi and I was happy for him.

I closed the door quietly and made my way over to my room.

Maybe Aaliya was waiting for me in my room.

I opened the door slowly, done with the quota of curses which I had received from every other room. That's when I saw something I otherwise would never have believed. My world would never be the same.

There was Aaliya, fully undressed, with Prerna, who was wearing nothing but her smile. They were kissing in the middle of my room. I realized in that moment how completely in love with Prerna I was. The whole time Prerna and I were playing games with each other to see who was attracted to whom, I saw that the game was only being played in my mind.

That annoyed the shit out of me. And Aaliya probably was never obtainable. She was never interested in either one of us, or DJ, or Shahrukh Khan for that matter.

Which brings me to the most important rule for today's time. *Ghor kalyug time.*

> **Rule 10: Find out if the girl is more interested in girls or guys? Use this rule before any other rule so that it saves you lot of time, money and beer.**

I have to say they looked great together. Oh, I know you're thinking that I am talking like an ass. But which guy would leave an opportunity to watch two hot girls making out.

Kya mast lag rahi thi yaar.

After wanting Aaliya for the last two weeks, I came to realize, after opening my bedroom door, that she wasn't what I wanted after all. *Angoor khattey nikley.*

I didn't give the girls a chance to notice me. I quietly closed the door and went back while they continued their holy ritual.

The bodies scattered all over the living room reduced my options. I had to find someone. I couldn't just sleep alone. What would my Bull say to me in the morning?

I looked around and stumbled into the kitchen. There she was. Ruchika…what was her last name?

I quietly observed her and realized she was pouring beer in a Maggi cup. I think she was hungry and planning to eat my signature dish. She bent over the kitchen counter as she filled the cup. The morning view was beautiful. I was amazed to see how she could figure out this special dish. Maybe we had a divine connection.

She turned around and smiled at me. I walked over to her and kissed her.

Maybe we were meant to be together. At least for tonight.